A REMOTE
BUT FREQUENTED
SHORE

To The Belg Family

By Robert Capone

Rat

D **P**

Dazé Publishing

Orange, California

Cover Art by Sergio A. Soto

Printed in the United States of America

ISBN   978-0-9785176-9-4

Attention Schools and Other Organizations:
Quantity discounts are available for this novel.
If you would like to purchase 20 or more of these
books, please contact Dazé Publishing via email.
Dazepublishing@yahoo.com

Chapter One
The Sarcasm of Destiny

Miguel awakened, Lourdes sleeping at his side. Having returned home only last night after three weeks at sea, the bed where he lay seemed to sway. Miguel tried to remain still in the cool of the Mazatlán morning as he studied the smooth curves of Lourdes' body. Her loving closeness brought healing to the bruises inflicted upon him by the sharp corners of the shrimp boat. In Lourdes' slumber Miguel rested from his toil; her comfort being his joy.

A small bird began to sing from a perch on the branch of a lime tree outside the open window of Miguel and Lourdes' bedroom. Miguel carefully turned his head and listened to the solitary chirping. When the song bird stopped, he cast his attention through the window beyond the lime tree to the tall brewing tower of *Pacifico Cerveza*. Then Miguel put the same question to himself that he had years before, the same question all the young men in Old Town Mazatlán ask themselves,

"Shall I be a fisherman or work at the brewery?" Miguel smiled, happy to be a fisherman, and roused Lourdes from sleep. She sighed and stretched in one movement from head to toe. Then he said to her,

"Sing for me, my morning dove."

Lourdes turned over and they made love.

Overcome by the heat of passion and the warming day, the cool morning stayed no longer. Lourdes pushed herself out of bed and stood before the mirror of her vanity. She parted and combed the brown hair that curled at her shoulders. Aware of Miguel's gaze, she slowly leaned over, reaching for a dress in her modest wardrobe.

"How can I be your Mexican Nightingale by night and your Morning Dove by day?" Lourdes asked. Miguel, too content to speak, pondered the question. Then he answered,

"Once you longed for me, now we're a pair."

Lourdes looked in the mirror with her blue eyes beaming. She smiled at her husband as she pulled some panties up to her wide hips and fastened a bra over her large breasts.

"If we have a little extra this month, can we go to the theater Saturday?" Lourdes asked.

"If I'm not fishing," Martin replied. Lourdes frowned and exclaimed,

"You're home only one night and all you can think of is that mistress of yours!"

"*Isabel* aches for me. She longs for me like a mermaid out of water," Miguel boasted.

"You'd rather be with that *lancha* than in bed with me. I'm jealous," Lourdes teased.

"Well, Friday is a full moon." Miguel paused. "If you let me spend the night in *Isabel* on Friday, I'd be happy to go to the theater with you on Saturday."

"You're on," Lourdes said as she finished dressing.

Miguel's thoughts remained with *Isabel*, his own beloved twenty-foot boat, named in honor of an aunt, until Lourdes, passing by, pulled the bed-sheet off him as she left the room.

The sight of the purplish-green bruises on his legs reminded Martin of the cause for his sore discoloration; the nameless shrimp boat on which he had worked for the last three weeks. He saw old tire bumpers dangling from the rusty sides as crewmen yelled back and forth across the deck. Miguel watched as his aching wrists twisted the heads off countless clear, beige and blue shrimps. He washed the small, medium and large tails in baskets and preserved them in cold, salty water in the refrigerated hold.

Miguel lowered the huge iron-sided pallets off each side of the shrimp boat from its spread *plumas*. The extension of these long metal arms from vertical to around fifteen degrees appeared like a bird with its wings spread out. Miguel waited with the crew as the pallets dragged along the sea floor. He imagined the shrimp, disturbed from the muddy bottom, trying a backward escape by thrusting their tails only to be caught in an onrushing net.

Then Miguel thought of their enemy, the crab, also taken by the net, seeing in his mind's eye the pinching claws severing the prized big blue shrimp. Miguel marveled at the irony: that the shrimp capital of the world would grant the crab such a prominent place on its municipal emblem. Mazatlán, at a latitude of 23 degrees 13 minutes north, is located just south of the tropic of cancer; and hence the zodiac sign of the crab on the city's crest.

A preemptory knock on the door brought Miguel back from the hard rusty boat to the comfort of his soft bed.

"Just a minute," Miguel responded as he reached for the bed-sheet to cover himself.

"Dad, breakfast is ready," rang the voice of one of his daughters.

"Be right there," Miguel replied. He smelled chorizo and heard the deliberate clunk of a plate and the carefree clang of a cup on the table beyond the bedroom door. Miguel, nostrils flaring to savor the aroma, leapt from bed, pulled on some shorts and opened the door. He walked a few steps and took his place at the head of the table in the center of his home.

The dining area was an extension of the kitchen, at one corner of the square house, which blended into the living area. The two other corners of the house featured a bedroom for the boys and another for the girls separated by the front door.

Miguel said a prayer over the food, gazed in gratitude over his three boys and three girls and reached for the chorizo and eggs. Lourdes poured sweet, fresh-squeezed orange juice from a glass pitcher.

"Mom, you're wearing your pearl earrings," Eloisa, the oldest daughter, remarked.

"Your father is taking me to the Angela Peralta Theater on Saturday," Lourdes replied. "I want to make sure my ears are still pierced so I can wear them." The small pearl earrings, Lourdes' only jewelry besides a wedding ring and necklace with a religious medal, were a gift from her mother garnered from the local oysters that make Mazatlán the *Pearl of the Pacific*.

"I'm studying about Angela Peralta in class," Eloisa said. Then she darted from the table to the girl's room asking, "Dad, may I be excused?"

"I'm taking *Isabel* out tonight and Friday," Miguel said with a look at his oldest son, Adam. "Who wants to join me?"

"Dad, take me fishing," Martin, Miguel's middle son, pleaded.

"You're not old enough yet," Adam, Martin's big brother, responded. "Dad, I'll go tonight but not Friday. There is a party tomorrow night."

"I'll be ten next month!" Martin stated.

Eloisa returned to the table and passed the tortillas to make room for her textbook. She began to read aloud:

"Angela Peralta was a child prodigy born in Mexico City. Before she reached twenty years of age her voice was heard in the opera houses of Madrid and Milan. The Spaniards called her the *Mexican Nightingale*. An adoring throng greeted her when she arrived at Mazatlán on a ship from San Francisco in August of 1883. They say that men vied with horses to have the privilege of pulling Ms. Peralta in a carriage to the hotel where she stayed. Upon arriving, she waved from her balcony to the fans below and then withdrew. But by the time *La Favorita*, the opera in which she starred, commenced, the director of the orchestra was already dead. Angela left earth's stage at the end of August. The curtain also closed on half the population of Mazatlán from a pandemic of the plague.

"Angela's premature departure was attributed by Francisco Gomez Flores, a Sinolese author, to *the sarcasm of destiny*."

Eloisa closed her textbook and slowly repeated the phrase,

"*The sarcasm of destiny*."

The words hung in the warm morning air.

Chapter Two
Heartland

Rodolfo climbed a narrow trail flanked by thorny brush, reached the top of a rocky mountain, and struggled to catch his breath through the dust. When his breathing settled, Rodolfo looked assertively upon his land in *Los Altos de Jalisco* and spit the dirt out of his mouth. A dry wind gusted over the brown terrain as the sun glinted off a watering hole in the valley below. Stooping toward the ground, Rodolfo picked up a dead stick and twirled it between his large hands, remembering the first time his father brought him to the top of the sacred mountain.

During the rainy season, the green valley had been dotted with golden ponds and speckled with roaming cattle. Rodolfo's father and his father's father had been *charros*, Mexican cowboys, the hardworking backbone of the heartland of his country. They had slaughtered cattle for beef and tanned hides for leather. Though Rodolfo still wore the boots and hat of his former trade, things had changed in his generation. The open range had become a pasture. He had turned his family ranch into a dairy farm.

In many ways, Rodolfo's family was dirt poor. The land they occupied was worth a fortune but the sustenance it provided was just enough to feed and clothe his fourteen children. Now, a powerful neighbor to the north coveted his land.

Following the contours of the valley, Rodolfo stood up and identified his aged stone house and old wooden barn in the distance. Evening approached and the cows needed milking. Having made his decision, he turned for home.

When Rodolfo arrived back at the barn, all the members of his family busied themselves with the evening chores. His oldest son, Israel, tied the large testicled steer to a post as his brothers and sisters kept the placid cows with swollen udders in a neat, though uneven, line. As the sun shone bright red-orange, the roosters crowed and the chickens paraded through the yard, and the hogs and pigs hovelled in their pens against the back wall of the stone house.

Rodolfo had left his concerns at the base of the sacred mountain and returned to his family in habitual cheerfulness. He winked at Magdalena, his wife, who nervously squeezed milk from a cow into a bucket. Hoping to reassure her, he hummed as he heaved a bale of hay into a trough. Rodolfo whistled at the first cow, now milked and fed, and swatted its hind quarter to make room for the next bovine.

Meanwhile, next to Rodolfo and his wife, Israel and his older sister Socorro followed the same routine as their parents. They worked together to avoid injury from a kicking hoof or delay from a frightened animal.

Israel, a strong and confident seventeen-year-old, more Spanish than Indian in appearance, spoke softly to the submissive stock even as he fantasized about a future apart from the dairy farm. He thought about what he would buy if his father sold the land. He imagined driving a car with Gisela, his newest girlfriend, at his side. He tried to push the thought out of his mind but it kept returning like a wayward calf as he traced a scar on top of his right hand.

"Israel," Socorro shouted from a stool. Hearing the voice, Israel swatted the cow away, poured the warm creamy milk from the bucket into a large canister, and led the next cow into place. Then Israel asked his dad,

"Can Joaquin and I go into town tomorrow night?"

"Mind your work, boy," Rodolfo responded. "We'll talk about it after supper."

During dinner in the stone house, Israel asked his dad again,

"Can Joaquin and I go into town tomorrow night?" This time Rodolfo answered,

"Yes, so long as your chores are done." Putting her fork down, Israel's mother, Magdalena, looked anxiously at her husband and added,

"Stay away from the Melendez boy."

Israel winked at his brother with flashing green eyes from across the table and said,

"Pass the beans." The excitement of a night out, the first in weeks, increased his appetite.

After the meal, Rodolfo sat in a chair and thought about his land and his family. The property adjacent to his on the other side of the sacred mountain changed hands the year before. A family of long standing sold it under questionable circumstances to Mr. Melendez, a member of the Mexican Mafia. Since then, Mr. Melendez repeatedly offered a fair price for his land. Rodolfo thanked him and refused each time, reiterating how dear the land was to him. Recently, threats began to reach his ears on visits to town.

Rodolfo looked at his three youngest daughters, the most beautiful of a handsome people. They gazed back at him from large brown eyes, made the more round by the shape of their dark eyebrows. They blinked at him innocently and continued playing their game. Then Rodolfo thought about his oldest sons; they had character but he wondered if their virtue had matured enough to protect them from the barrage of temptations in town.

Later, when the rest of the family gathered on the mismatched sofas in the living room, Rodolfo reached for one of the two books he owned. The volume he grasped was not the Bible but a biography of Hernan Cortés, the Spanish conquistador of Mexico. He read aloud:

> "Cortés appealed to the courage and sense of honor in his men saying, 'Do you not value dying with honor more than living without honor?'"

Rodolfo left the book open on his lap and looked at Israel and Joaquin. Then he asked in a firm voice,

"Boys, what is courage?"

"Courage is standing up to fight for your family and friends, for what you believe in, even to the point of death" Israel, the oldest son, responded.

"Sounds heroic," Rodolfo smiled. "Courage is doing what you know is right, even when you are afraid. But did Cortés always fight? No. He knew what he wanted and he choose the right means for achieving it. He avoided battles and made alliances."

"Dad, you can't always talk your way out of arguments. Sometimes you have to fight!" Israel protested.

"You might fight and win a battle but still lose the war. The prudent man looks where he is going. Sometimes the courageous thing to do is to turn the other cheek."

Rodolfo finished speaking and studied Joaquin. The boy, a big sixteen-year old full of bravado, was already among the strongest men in town. Rodolfo realized, especially with Israel's influence, that Joaquin would not suffer an insult quietly nor shrink from a fight.

Uncomfortable with the scrutiny directed at him by his father, Joaquin asked,

"Dad, tell us about Victoriano Catorce again."

"Victoriano was a *Cristero* and a great uncle of yours. He was called to the town of San Miguel to protect the people and prevent a church from being taken by the *Pelones*. Fourteen soldiers on horseback surrounded Victoriano. He fell to the ground, six-shooters blazing, and fought his way out alive. Rising victorious, he removed a holy medal from under his tongue and exclaimed, 'Viva La Virgen de San Juan, she is with me and the church.'"

The history of the family filled Rodolfo and his sons with a strength based on confidence. They did not court danger but neither did they run from threats. They learned early, like every man eventually does, the vast gap between the first antagonistic word and the first punch. But living in-between these overtures for so long brought unease to the family.

Chapter Three
Gray Dawn

Miguel and Lourdes walked amidst the spray from The Fishermen's Monument in Mazatlán. To them, the fountain was devoted to the theme of comings and goings. They looked at the sculptured features of a young bronze man holding a matted fishing net. His thick hair blew in one direction, on shore, a majestic billed fish at his feet. High above, a tiled lighthouse made its circular rounds. A descending arc from the lighthouse became the hammock on which lay a representation of home, a beautiful woman in the throws of agony or ecstasy. Miguel and Lourdes couldn't agree if she was feeling the anguish of waiting for the return of her man or the pleasure of reunion with him.

The fountain expressed their deepest hopes and fears, brought them to the surface, and made saying "I'll miss you" or "Come back safe" unnecessary. They simply stood below the fountain, enjoying the same spray of water that burst from the sculpted image into the reflective pool.

"Ready to turn back?" Miguel asked his wife.

"Only if you take me the long way."

Lourdes walked slowly. Miguel looked at the full moon rising in the evening sky. They followed the promenade, passing Ice Box Hill, Lookout Hill, and the ferry to La Paz. Miguel's pace quickened as the moon brightened. Finally, they paralleled the cruise line and naval dock and turned to climb a short hill aimed at the *Pacifico Cerveza* brewing tower. When they reached home, Lourdes gave Miguel a kiss on the cheek and they embraced.

After leaving Lourdes, but before reaching the water and *Isabel*, Miguel stopped off at his brother Benjamin's house. He was informed that Benjamin had already left for the night in another boat. He gently berated himself for not having made arrangements earlier for someone to join him. His concern and sense of loneliness lasted a few seconds. Then he looked at the moon again and knew that the Sierra and Corbina would rise to it. Miguel, stimulated by the adventure ahead, smiled. He hoped to return to the fish market with his catch by four in the morning. Then he would rinse the smooth white sides and light blue interior of his *lancha*.

Miguel did not see any stars in the clear night sky as he sat in the stern of *Isabel*. He motored by the world's tallest lighthouse set atop a cavernous mountain that marks the entrance to Mazatlán's port. Now, fully realizing he entered the ocean alone, he told himself of the importance of remaining attentive for tankers and to take care in his own activities. Looking over his shoulder, Miguel felt comfort at seeing the lit yellow-tiled bell towers of the Cathedral. The bishop and his canons visited the docks in September and blessed the boats. Martin could still remember the gist of the prayer:

> God of boundless love, at the beginning of creation your Spirit hovered over the deep.
> You called forth every creature,
> and the seas teemed with life.
> Through your Son, Jesus Christ, you have given us the rich harvest of salvation.
> Bless this boat, its equipment and all who will use it.

Protect them from the dangers of wind and rain and all the perils of the deep.

May Christ, who calmed the storm and filled the nets of his disciples,

Bring us all to the harbor of light and peace.

Becoming lost at sea was a danger. Miguel navigated by sight, even at night. There was no compass or radio on board his *lancha*. He took his bearings from the guano-covered Two Brothers islands that shone white in the moonlight and headed for Goat, Deer and Bird islands.

Miguel thought of the explorer, Vizcaino, who described Mazatlán as the *port of islands* as he navigated the Sinaloa coast. He also remembered that those on land called Mazatlán the *place of ciervos* from the Nahutal Indian word *mazatl*, meaning the place of deer.

Isabel leapt like a gazelle over the small swells as Miguel's smile bound across his face with the ocean breeze. After an hour he glided to a stop in a secret spot.

"How quiet it is," he thought, "without the voice of a friend or the hum of the motor." Little waves licked the side of the *lancha* as he prepared his lines. There was neither rod nor reel to assemble, just hands to warm.

Miguel decided by primitive instinct to fish by hand. He could have set the float and eased his net adrift behind, but the other method was more effective. He tied a hook and sinker with sure knots. A small, brown, live shrimp was his bait. He had no need for a measured heave but let the weight do its work. Line passed through his fingers into the depths below.

Miguel's thumbs and fingers poised for a strike. Reflex clamped them together with the first bite. He began pulling his prize in hand over hand and landed a good-sized Corbina.

With the first fish Miguel gently derided himself for so many of his earlier trepidations.

"No large waves, no high winds to worry about. The odds of a tangle with a manta or whale are slim." He checked to make sure the light atop of the stern pole was on to alert bigger ships of his presence. Then he warned himself,

"Don't get haughty."

Miguel felt a little proud and very lucky as he continued to catch fish. He had many Corbina and a few Sierra. Then the fish stopped biting.

"Did a larger fish spook you?" he said to the fish as if they were friends. Then he felt for his pocketknife to be sure it was in his front pocket. "I don't need a big fish. These are fine," Miguel thought, so as not to acknowledge his apprehensions about hooking a big fish, so dangerous to those who work by hand.

Miguel settled himself uneasily onto a cushion and waited with attentive hands.

"Stay awake," he told himself. "Keep your hands apart." He checked the moon and steadied his hands. Then sleep slowly crept over him like the imperceptibility of the passing planets. Miguel's hands relaxed into his lap. The line that had been kept straight and taut loosely coiled. A loop now formed around the middle and pinky fingers of his left hand.

Suddenly the feared large fish struck and the coiled loop tightened. Miguel jolted to attention with the quick movement and growing discomfort. He looked at his swelling digits with alarm and reached for his pocketknife. Just then the strong fish pulled with such force that the edge of the sharp line severed three of his fingers.

"Could this be happening to me," he thought as blood gushed forth from his hand and trickled down his arm in scarlet rivulets. It all seemed to be happening in slow motion. Miguel's mind raced. "Keep it elevated. Make a tourniquet. Grab that rag." His right hand wrapped the cloth around his elbow. He placed one end between his teeth and pulled as tightly as he could.

Miguel had lost a lot of blood. He tried to start the engine but could not with only one hand. He felt cold, weak, dizzy and sick. He breathed with shallow irregularity. He mumbled,

"Into your hands Lord, I commend my spirit" and hoped he might hold on until dawn. He saw the lighthouse before his eyes shut.

The first rays of a lavender dawn shone over Old Town Mazatlán. The small waves slowly pushed *Isabel* toward Fishermen's Monument and *Los Pinos* Beach. The bleeding had stopped but Miguel was dead.

Chapter Four
Ambush in Jalisco

Israel and Joaquin left their father's aged stone house in *Los Altos de Jalisco*. They strutted side by side down the dark and dusty road leading to town. The brothers moved with an alacrity borne on the air of Friday night anticipation, their posture punctuated by the pride of youth. Together they felt invincible, ready to take the town by audacious cunning or concupiscent charm.

Joaquin's friends called him "baby face" for his pudgy cheeks and shy smile. His acquaintances described him as a gentle giant, even at sixteen years of age. Joaquin's strength astounded Israel, who used to fight his younger brother until the day in their twelfth and thirteenth year when they both discovered that Joaquin could prevail. Henceforth, neither brother sought a tangle with the other again.

The twinkling of the stars stopped and the electric lights intensified as the brothers reached the outskirts of the small town after a two mile's walk. A beer-can rolled off the pavement and came to a stop ahead of them where the road narrowed. The brothers took the sidewalk for the last few blocks to the town's square.

"Israel, over here," hailed a familiar voice holding out a beer from a parked car that pulsed with *Ranchero* music on the plaza's edge. Israel opened the can, placed a boot on the chrome front bumper of the car, and posed for the girls who paraded in a continuous semi-circle within the parameters of the square under the watchful eyes of their chaperones.

"Hey baby face, you want a beer? You open it with that tab on top." Laughter erupted around the parked car as more of the town's young men gravitated to Israel. Soon the girls stopped and talked with the boys.

Among the ladies was Israel's girlfriend, Gisela. She wore a red dress with lace. She made the dress herself and had written to Israel about wearing it for him.

On the opposite side of the plaza, Orlando Melendez sat in his jacked-up four-by-four snorting a line of cocaine. Rubbing his nose, he opened a beer and watched Israel gesticulate with his arms across the square.

"They're laughing at me. Let's go," Orlando Melendez commanded.

"Not now, there are too many of them," a voice from the back of the extended cab objected.

"Nobody's going to touch us. I'll take him right now!"

Orlando Melendez, pompously groomed, jumped from his jacked-up truck and crossed the square hurriedly with his three reluctant friends. They beat a path through the people to Israel.

"What are you doing off the farm?" Melendez asked. Israel took his boot off the bumper and faced Melendez eye to eye.

"The only tits you'll get your hands on are found on the farm," Melendez said with a derogatory tone to the winces of the young women. Gisela shied away, particularly embarrassed by the comment and concerned that it might entangle Israel in a feud with a mafia boss's son.

"I've been coming here all my life," Israel replied.

"You won't for long if you keep calling me a rump ranger."

Joaquin, standing at his brother's side, laughed and repeated the phrase as a question, *"rump ranger"*? Orlando Melendez pushed Joaquin as hard as he could. Joaquin, unmoved, brushed off the push as more laughter cracked through the tension. Israel, becoming serious, asked,

"Who said I called you *that*?"

Orlando looked around at the faces that stared back at him and responded desperately,

"Everyone."

"Who?" Israel asked again.

"Stay out of my way," Orlando Melendez said, leaving to go.

"Let's stay out of each other's way," Israel said with a conciliatory edge. Orlando turned on the phrase rapidly and punched Israel in the stomach. Israel doubled over, out of breath. In retaliation, Joaquin instantly threw a punch that landed on Orlando's eye, knocking him to the ground. No one moved.

Orlando's reluctant friends held their palms out in front of their chests in a gesture that indicated they had enough. Each secretly felt Melendez needed to be brought down as they picked him up and retreated across the square to the four-by-four. The truck revved loudly and someone standing close to Israel warned jovially,

"Watch out, he'll probably try to off-road it through the plaza and run us all down."

Israel and Joaquin smiled cautiously at each other as the four-by-four stormed away.

Israel felt the chemistry within his own body change as he reached for his girlfriend's hand. The adrenaline dissipated through the square as his hormones harmonized with the plaza.

"Drive Joaquin home when you leave tonight."

"Okay," responded the voice of Israel's friend from the car.

"What about you?" Joaquin asked.

"I can watch out for myself," Israel reprimanded.

Later, after midnight, Israel, still a little inebriated, left the small town along what now felt like a lonely road. He didn't mind the cover provided by the heavy darkness as he looked haphazardly over his shoulder. After awhile he could see the fence post marking the place where the dirt of the road and that of the driveway to the farmhouse merged. He walked through the door and found the bedroom he shared with Joaquin in the dark. The waiting Joaquin greeted him,

"What happened with Gisela?"

"We talked in the plaza and went to her house. Her parents wouldn't even let me put my arm around her."

"Your reputation preceded you?"

"My reputation? That was some punch you threw tonight."

"I thought you were mad," Joaquin said.

"I just wish it hadn't turned out that way," Israel said wearily.

"You're not going to tell dad are you?" Joaquin asked tentatively.

"I won't have to. The whole town is still talking about it."

"What should we do?"

"Dad won't mind, so long as we are up and working in the morning. Good night."

"Good night," Joaquin responded. Joaquin was still awake as Israel's snoring began, thinking about the punch that sent Melendez to the ground.

A few hours later, Joaquin heard the roosters wake the dawn. He shook Israel and whispered over the snoring,

"Get up, get up."

Soon, they were both in the wooden barn, leading the cows to their milking stations. Joaquin watched one of his little sisters run down to a nearby pond for water as the sun rose over the mountains. Joaquin worked as his dad approached. Joaquin wondered what he would say if his dad asked about last night.

"Good morning," Rodolfo said, greeting his son.

"Chewy isn't eating," yelled one of Joaquin's sisters.

"Good morning," Joaquin replied. Then he watched out of the corner of his eye as his dad checked on one of the cows. Joaquin continued observing his dad until Rodolfo was slowly absorbed by the morning chores.

Leading the last of the cows out of the barn, Joaquin stood up and stretched. Suddenly, he was ambushed by four of his littlest brothers and sisters. They came from a corner of the barn, from the house and from a hill by the pond. Joaquin laughed as two of the children hung from his neck; one clutched a leg and the other an arm.

"You can do better than that," he said with warm encouragement and hilarity. Then he fell to the ground, not knowing how, and felt hands squeezing at his ticklish sides. Israel appeared above him laughing and said,

"Time for breakfast."

"Let's get those canisters of milk to the side of the road for pickup first," Joaquin said, trying to delay a conversation with his dad that might uncover last night's shenanigans.

"Okay. I'll use the two-wheeler and bring the canisters halfway up from the barn. You take them the rest of the way to the fencepost."

"Why do you get the dolly?"

"It will only roll over the level ground near the barn. The ground is too rough and uneven near the end of the driveway. Besides, there are only five of them," Israel replied. "You'll have to carry them. When all the canisters are halfway, I'll help you carry the rest to the fencepost. We'll see if you can carry two at a time. Agreed?"

"Agreed," Joaquin said, relishing a new threshold for a demonstration of his strength.

Joaquin smiled with satisfaction to himself, resting at the halfway point, until Israel dropped off the first canister of milk with the hand-truck. Joaquin concentrated, bent down to use his legs as his dad had taught him, rocked the narrow but tall canister to one side making room at the bottom for his hand, and lifted the milk onto his shoulder. Then he walked the twenty yards from the halfway point to the fencepost and set the canister down.

Two young men crouched in a trench on the opposite side of the dirt road where it curved out of sight. Orlando Melendez, taking aim with one eye swollen shut, held a shotgun and said,

"I'm going to wait and shoot them both."

Joaquin turned back toward the barn and another canister met him at the halfway point, his brother already on the way with a third. This time he rocked the canister and hoisted it to his opposite shoulder, thinking the muscles on each side of his body should share the labor and rewards. He carried the load to the fencepost, wiped his brow and turned back to the barn. As he approached the midway point, he saw his brother standing over two canisters, pointing at them with a broad grin.

"You are warmed up now. Let's see if you can haul two of these things from here to the fence post. You ready?" Israel asked.

"Yes," Joaquin replied as he methodically rocked the first canister and lifted it to his shoulder. "You're going to have to help me get the second one to my shoulder."

Israel tilted the canister over but it fell and rolled a few feet on its side. Israel tried again, looking at his brother who did not seem to mind the delay. Tilting the canister with more concentration, Israel lifted it up and placed it onto his brother's shoulder.

"I've got it. If I make it, you won't tell dad about last night?"

"Don't worry about last night," Israel responded.

Joaquin turned toward the road. Israel watched his brother, and, knowing he would make it to the fencepost, turned for the last canister in the barn.

Walking carefully over the uneven ground, Joaquin approached the lone fence post with rusted and snarled barbed wire hanging from one side. His hands cradled the round canisters on top of his shoulders. He felt the weight dig into his trapezoids. Nonetheless, he smiled through grit teeth, knowing he would make it to the roadside.

On the other side of the street, Orlando aimed his double-barreled shotgun at Joaquin's exposed chest from his place in the gutter.

Reaching the fencepost at the roadside, Joaquin paused, wondering how he would get both canisters to the ground without hurting himself.

Orlando Melendez pulled the trigger of the shotgun twice, the shells leaving the barrels with a blast.

Joaquin's arms fell to his sides, the metal canisters slamming to the ground, his chest exploding with pain.

Chapter Five
The Water's Edge

Lourdes moved through the Cathedral doors with a spring in her step and joy in her heart. She celebrated the 6:30 morning Mass and was on her way to the Central Market. Miguel, her husband, was probably home from fishing and sleeping by now, she thought. Lourdes wanted to prepare a special midday meal for her family.

Mazatalán's Central Market, established in the middle of the nineteenth century, felt like an Italian train station for its echoic sound and diffuse lighting. Under the high tin roof people moved along the aisles like trains over tracks between the stationary platforms from which produce, poultry, beef, dairy and sweets were sold.

Lourdes had a few extra pesos to splurge on her shopping. The butcher cut her the beef for a roast. She replenished her supplies of fresh onions and dried peppers. The confectioner sliced her a few pieces of membrillo from a brown jelly-like mold as a pineapple poked at her side. After the baker placed some fresh bread in a bag, Lourdes could carry no more. She left the market and took a bus to the *colonia* where her family lived.

Lourdes arrived home to hugs and kisses. The girls took the grocery bags off her hands and started putting the food away.

"Dad's not home yet," Martin said.

"Oh. Why don't you go to the dock and see if you can find him," Lourdes said with a little concern. Martin felt happy to go. His mother would not have a chance to dream up a Saturday morning chore for him to do. He also liked taking his dad's three-wheeled yellow bike for a spin.

Martin cruised down a short hill and stopped to walk Miguel's bike across the busy avenue. Then he peddled a little farther to a dirt lot filled with old cars that gave way to a fish market. He looked for his father near the water's edge where hungry pelicans walked with webbed feet, looking dignified until they fluttered for scraps of fish, the nape of their brown and white haired necks standing up comically.

Martin saw a few familiar faces and asked if anyone had seen his dad that morning.

"I saw your dad leave alone last night," one fisherman said. "He was going toward Goat Island."

"Why would dad go there?" Martin asked himself.

"Shucks, if I were older dad would have taken me fishing last night," Martin shrugged, thinking about the approach of his tenth birthday.

Hopping on the yellow bike, Martin peddled down *Zaragoza* Avenue and turned onto *Cinco de Mayo*. He took a few short-cuts down a maze of colorful colonial facades and arrived at the beach just south of The Fishermen's Monument. He was breathing heavily from the exertion and a few near-misses with the *Pulmonieas*, Mazatlán's open air taxis.

Martin looked at the beach that served as an embarcadero for *lanchas*, a few of which laid bottoms up on the sand. This seemed a reverent way and place for an old boat to find rest after carrying its passengers over the sea so faithfully through the years.

"Have you seen *Isabel?*" Martin asked.

"Which one, boy?" a sun-drenched fisherman asked gruffly. "*Isabel I, II or III?*" he laughed.

To Martin there was only, could only be, one *Isabel*.

"My dad's *Isabel*," Martin replied with all the manhood he could muster.

"No, I haven't, son. But there are many boats returning now. See um?"

Martin looked at the widely spaced single-file line of *lanchas* coming over the water toward the landing from Goat, Deer and Bird Islands.

"My dad went out last night," Martin groaned. For the first time it occurred to him that his dad might be in trouble. Riding on, Martin followed the *Olas Atlas* promenade past *Los Pinos* Beach. From his new vantage point his young bright eyes detected a single boat, moving slowly, more than a mile away. The *lancha* looked empty. He could not see the usual half-silhouetted figures seated at bow and stern.

Martin turned for home peddling even faster with a lump in his throat. He walked through the front door, relieved to see his older brother.

"Mom was just sending me out to look for you and dad. Where's dad?" Adam asked.

"No one has seen him," Martin said between breaths with his hands on his knees.

"What?"

"No one has seen him since last night. He was going to the islands alone."

"Alone?" Adam asked, remembering that his dad had asked him to join him. Adam did not go because he had a date with his friends. He figured his dad would find someone else; he always did, because everybody liked him and he was lucky.

"You stay here. I'm going to get uncle and find dad," Adam ordered, already at the door.

"Adam?"

"Yeah?"

"I saw a boat from *Los Pinos*. It was moving slowly out
at sea, going south. I think it might be *Isabel*," Martin paused, a
clear tear in one of his grey-blue eyes, and continued,

"There's no one in it."

"Don't mention that to mom. We'll find dad," Adam said
before he shut the door behind him.

Lourdes' nerves stiffened with the passing hours. She
took the night's frayed theater tickets from her apron pocket and
rubbed them nostalgically between her fingers. She reached for
her earrings and touched the little, hard pearls. Her kitchen,
usually a blissful place where the cooking couldn't be heard over
the talking, was crackling, pounding and cutting in the quiet.
Martin sat one moment waiting for the door knob to turn and then
got up the next to look out the window.

Forked-tailed Frigate birds circled high above *Isabel*
making her easy to find. Pelicans stood on her sides as a few
gulls hovered near the stern. Adam and his uncle slowed as the
approach became more difficult to cope with. They pulled
alongside *Isabel* and found Miguel slumped over in the stern.

"Oh, Jesus," Benjamin, Adam's uncle and Miguel's
brother, kept saying. Both thought vaguely about how they
would tell their mother the news.

"Adam, lay out the net and take a few blankets from my
boat," Benjamin said. Meanwhile, he scooped his brother's
congealed blood mixed with water over the side as he thought
about what to do next.

"Oh, Jesus," Benjamin said again as he took Miguel's cap
off his head and stuffed it into a pocket. Then he removed his
brother's clothes and sponged his body with the cleanest cloth he
could find.

Adam and Benjamin struggled to lay the dead weight out straight over the fishing net. They wrapped a towel around Miguel's waist and used another one to cover his body.

"Do you think you can lead us home?" Benjamin asked, appealing to the hero in Adam.

"Yes."

"Take it slow."

Adam piloted his uncle's boat while Benjamin followed in *Isabel* with Miguel's body. He wanted to sob out loud but there was too much yet to do.

Martin and Adam entered the harbor with a marine escort. By the time they reached the dock a few *lanchas* flanked *Isabel*. All attention was focused on her. Everyone on the water's edge sensed death.

The morbid murmur spread quickly through the *colonia* but silence shrouded the street where Miguel had lived. Inside, lunch was ready but Lourdes was reluctant to serve it until Miguel returned home.

"Knock, Knock."

"Ring, Ring."

The door knob turned. The moment Martin saw his brother's face he knew that his dad was dead. He started to cry. Benjamin asked Lourdes to sit on the couch. Adam gathered the family. Benjamin reached for Miguel's fishing cap and pocket knife and handed them to Lourdes.

The girls started to cry out loud and tears fell silently from the boys' eyes. Other family members wailed and soon friends poured in and out of the home from the neighboring streets. When Miguel's mother arrived, Benjamin took her and Lourdes by the hand and led them to the shore of the sea. Columns of people formed along the way. Hushed silence, mumbled songs and loud petitions accompanied the solemn procession.

A priest waited at the water's edge, ready to lead the prayers for the dead. Miguel floated on *Isabel* as Benjamin had left him, though the cloth that had covered him was removed to the waist, the hand with the missing fingers hidden.

The funeral took place on a Tuesday in the Cathedral. The bishop presided. Martin was poor but well-known and liked. Moreover, his wife Lourdes, faithful in prayer and dependable in her ministries, sewed and altered the vestments. The homily made reference to Miguel's baptism into the death of Christ.

"Even though he was baptized," the bishop said, "he still suffered from sin and death. We all remember how our hearts sank when we heard the sad news of Miguel's death. But death does not have the last word. Let your hearts take strength in the Good News; Christ saves us from death and brings us into the safe harbor of his risen life in heaven."

Everyone heard the bishop but no one listened. Just as Miguel died suddenly of shock, the people were stunned by despair. The ritual of the Roman Catholic Church washed over the community with a familiar comfort. The incense burned, cantors sang and people cried, despite the flowers. They preferred to mourn now and hope later.

Lourdes' family was not the same after the loss of husband and father but continued with a resiliency stronger than death. Lourdes' faith only grew deeper. Adam dropped out of school, and, at sixteen, assumed the duties of protector and provider. Martin, the most sullen, didn't realize he carried the anger of the family.

Martin did not know he was mad at God, but he sure had a few questions for the bishop. He who had been the apple of his father's eye now felt strangely alone. He took his hurt out on others by asking questions that made them uncomfortable.

"Mom, why did God take dad away from us?"

"Adam, if the bishop blessed *Isabel*, why did dad die at sea?"

Lourdes could only answer, "I don't know."

Adam's response was always the same,

"The bishop blessed the boat and *Isabel* retuned, didn't she?"

Lourdes took out her worry over Martin on a needle and thread. Finally the black jacket and trousers were complete. While Martin was at school, she placed the suit out on his bed. They were going to see the bishop.

Chapter Six
Vengeance is Mine

Rodolfo heard the shotgun blast echo with horror off the sacred mountain of his ancestors. He dashed out of the aged stone house and saw Israel running from the old wooden barn toward the dirt road with a rifle. Then his oldest son stopped near the fencepost.

Israel had pushed the hand-truck with the last canister of milk, watching his brother reach the road with two canisters on his shoulders. Then he saw Joaquin fall to the ground and heard a blast. He could see two figures running from the fencepost toward town. Israel bolted to the barn for his dad's rifle.

When Israel reached the fencepost he stopped and knelt near Joaquin. His brother laid face down in the dust near some short brown grass, two milk canisters strewn, one to each side of his body. The cracked ground soaked up the blood that pooled around Joaquin's sides.

Setting the rifle against the splintered post with rusted barbed wire, Israel turned Joaquin's upper body, and then his lower body. Joaquin's pudgy cheeks were already sullen, his eyes closed, his nose and forehead chalky from the earth, everything else red with blood.

Feeling powerless, Israel reached for the rifle making ready to chase the killers down and avenge his brother's murder. Before he could stand, he felt his dad's hand on his shoulder.

"Leave it for now, son. Help me carry your brother to the barn."

Israel looked up into his dad's tearful eyes and set the rifle back on the fencepost. Rodolfo carried Joaquin's legs at the knees while Israel lifted his brother from under his arms. The other children circled their dad and brother during the dreadful chore, afraid to come too close. The older girls sobbed out-loud and ran to the stone house to tell their mother.

A hot wind gusted through the treeless valley. Israel's arms, back and legs burned under the dead weight of his brother. Rodolfo needed to stop for a rest, too, as the last of Joaquin's blood dripped to the dust. Both of their steps grew shorter, their feet shuffling hurriedly, as they reached the wooden barn. Only then did they set the body to the ground. There were no tables or benches but the old timbers of the barn roof provided shade.

"Fill the bucket, son," Rodolfo said, as he reached for an unraveled rope leading to a bell at the top of the barn. The drone of the alarm bell, carried by the hot wind, traveled miles through the rocky hillsides and down each side of the valley summoning the cousins and uncles who inhabited the neighboring ranches and farms.

Returning from the pond with a bucket of water, Israel stood motionless by his dad, who had removed his brother's tattered shirt, exposing the fatal wounds on his chest.

"Help me clean him up for his mother," Rodolfo said, as his other daughters and sons looked on from the open side of the barn.

By the time the body had been washed, a few of the relatives who lived closest to Rodolfo's farm arrived out of breath, rifles strung over their shoulders. They gazed silently at their nephew's and cousin's cratered chest. Before they could ask what happened Rodolfo said,

"Go to town and call for the priest."

Father Marcos arrived a few hours later, clothed in a black cassock and a white collar. Informed that Joaquin had been killed, Father Marcos prayed for the family on his way to Rodolfo's farm. He crossed the threshold of the stone house and entered a room filled with quiet mourners. A sturdy, oak grandfather clock seemed to carry the burden of time as its dials moved around a grey face to the tic and tock of a heavy pendulum.

Some of the family sat on the mismatched couches, others on a bed that had been brought into the room, while many stood against the wall. Everyone's eyes rested on Joaquin's body, now dressed in a white button-down shirt and black slacks. The corpse was laid out on a table next to the only windowed wall of the room from which shone the last rays of the setting sun.

Joaquin's mother was not aware of the priest's entry into the room until he stood in front of her son's body. Then she began to cry loudly with intermittent moans. Father Marcos walked to the grieving mother who sat on a couch. Magdalena looked up momentarily and didn't speak. Father Marcos picked up her inert hand in a gesture of condolence.

Rodolfo entered the room from a hallway and walked to Father Marcos. He received a short embrace and then whispered in the priest's ear,

"Father, please come with me." As they walked down the hallway of the stone house, Rodolfo informed the priest,

"Joaquin was shot. We think it is the Melendezes," Rodolfo said as he trained a shaggy black eyebrow with the quick and continuous strokes of his thumb. "I'm angry but these boys seek revenge. Tell them, tell them."

Before Father Marcos could ask, "Tell them what?" he was ushered into a small, darker room. His eyes adjusted and he tried to read the downcast faces of Israel, his fifteen-year-old brother Abel, two cousins and an uncle.

"My condolences," Father Marcos said. Silence was the response. Then the priest saw a crucifix hanging on a wall and continued,

"I feel like we are disciples at the foot of the cross. You remember, there was Mary, the mother of Jesus, and a few others who wept. Gaze upon the crucifix. What do you see?"

The downcast faces looked upon the crucifix. Israel saw the drops of blood, and the face seemed, for a moment, to be that of his brother, Joaquin. He rubbed his eyes, glanced at the crucifix again, and then looked down. Father Marcos continued,

"I see Jesus, so powerless, so vulnerable, suffering in pain, killed violently on the cross. I feel powerless and abandoned too. Here, arms nailed to the cross, the Son of God, the all-powerful one, handing himself over to men. I think he is asking us to let the violence end here. Our suffering savior says let the violence end here. What do you think?"

The men responded with silence.

"How do you think Mary felt, at the foot of the cross? Would you cause your grieving mother more pain by being locked up or buried like your brother will be tomorrow?" The priest tried to study the men's faces.

"I recall the words of scripture," Father Marcos said, "vengeance is mine, vengeance belongs to the Lord!" These words, it seemed to the priest, resonated more with the men right now. "Do you have the faith to leave the killer's punishment to the Lord? Do you have the love to save your mother any more pain? Do you have the holy fear of God to leave vengeance to the Lord and let the violence end here?"

The men looked at the priest with hesitation.

"I want an answer from each of you," Father Marcos commanded. Then, training his gaze on one man at a time, he waited for a mumbled yes and an affirmative nod before looking into the eyes of the next person.

Israel, his brother, cousins and an uncle all agreed to forego the blood feud of a vendetta and leave the punishment to the Lord. They were dismissed by Rodolfo, who led Father Marcos back down the hall to the room where Joaquin's body rested. By the light of candles, the priest began speaking the prayers for the dead from a small book with red and yellow ribbons. Israel squeezed onto the end of a couch next to one of his little sisters.

The candle wax melted in spindly shapes as the priest concluded a litany of tear-filled petitions. He closed his small prayer book and opened his hands over one, and then another member of the family.

Israel became rigid as the priest stood with outstretched hands above the little sister who sat beside him. Israel looked straight ahead at Joaquin's body and traced the scar on top of his clinched right hand and then lost himself in an upright flame, now bent coldly by a breeze passing through the window.

Feeling the push of the priest's palms on his head, Israel's chin lowered in supplication. Slowly, a gentle peace and abiding power filled his heart. Tears dropped into his open hands. The next thing Israel heard was his mother, who yelled,

"No, no!"

Father Marcos slowly drew his hands away.

"No, no," Magdalena yelled once more. Rodolfo tried to hold his wife but she shook and turned away. After a few moments, the priest, still standing in front of Magdalena, lowered his hands and placed them gently over her head. Crying, Magdalena placed her face on her husband's chest.

The melted candles on the table and floor around Joaquin's body were replaced before they burnt out. Israel carried the sister, who slept at his side, to bed, and placed her next to the other children. He hardly noticed the neighbors, who stationed themselves in the kitchen, cooking.

No member of the family was left alone. Women prayed the rosary inside the house as the men paced with rifles outside. Life continued in the same way for nine days, only interrupted by the funeral. On the tenth day, the novena complete and all the neighbors gone, Rodolfo called Israel into the living room.

Picking up the biography of Hernan Cortés, Rodolfo read aloud about the conquistador's sad escape from the Aztec capital and subsequent return and struggle to take the city of Mexico. Closing the book, Rodolfo said,

"I want you to take it with you." Israel held the book handed to him by his father in the suspended space between them.

"It's too dangerous for you to stay here now, but in time you will be able to return," Rodolfo said. "There is an envelope in the book with some money."

Israel brought the book closer as his father let go, and took the envelope, holding the money he had always coveted.

"It would please me if you devoted some of your resources to study. You'll also write to your mother," Rodolfo said. Israel nodded and looked at his father with an amalgam of sorrow and gratitude as marbled as his hazel-green eyes.

"Where will you go?" Rodolfo asked.

"Guadalajara," Israel responded.

For the second time in two weeks, Rodolfo's little girls cried at the departure of another beloved brother. Six months later Israel received a letter from his father.

November, 1990

Dear Son,
Our prayers have been answered. You can come home
now. The Melendezes have not only left town but are
leaving Jalisco. I wrote, telling you how Mr. Fernandez
wouldn't even sell them any groceries at the store after
your brother's death. Soon it was the same all over town.
No one would talk to them. Their land is deserted and
they are gone. Your mom awaits your return and we can
use your help on the farm.
Love, Dad.

Israel folded the letter, relieved for the safety of his
family, knowing he would not give up the bustling city for a
return to the dairy farm.

Chapter Seven
A Visit with The Bishop

Martin looked down and out across the checkerboard of black and white marble squares that make up the floor of the cathedral in Mazatlán. He felt like a pawn against fate.

And if life is anything like the game of chess, then his mother was queen. Lourdes interpreted life as a struggle between the forces of good and evil. She was well equipped to vanquish the foe. Today, however, she sought the help of the bishop to defend her son, who was like an isolated pawn under attack.

The bishop, for his part, played the center and kept watch over the rank and file along the diagonal of sound doctrine. He knew himself to be a servant of the Word in the tradition from which scripture was inspired. He taught, could only teach, that which had been handed on. He listened to it devoutly, guarded it scrupulously and explained it faithfully, always with the help of the Holy Spirit.

Lourdes and Martin made their move. They were greeted by a kind religious sister when they entered the cathedral's parish office and led up a flight of intimidating stairs. After the ascent, the sister said,

"Please take a seat, the bishop will see you shortly." Then she disappeared behind a door at the end of a long corridor. Lourdes checked the buttons on Martin's shirt and adjusted his

38

collar. Martin stared down at his swinging shoelaces, feeling like judgment had already been made on his young life and the punishment was about to be administered.

Then, from another direction, a high and narrow portal swung open and the sound of deliberate footsteps approached Lourdes and Martin. A man with the deportment of a butler politely asked for names and, confirming who the visitors were, said,

"Good. Good. The bishop will see you now."

Lourdes and Martin were ushered into the bishop's office, an alcove of the cathedral church. A yellow-tiled *cupola* ornately shone through a large window. Golden light beamed through parted red velvet curtains onto dark and finely grained furniture. The bishop's dark brown face and textured skin on a sturdy frame resembled the table and chairs. And just as Christ was nailed to the wood of the Cross, so the bishop was tied to the wood of his desk.

The bishop could hear the activity from the streets below but rarely set foot on their stones, so frequent and many were his visitors. The setting reinforced the feeling of being firmly in the world but not of the world. Yet like his master, the bishop did not need anyone to tell him about human nature, he knew it well.

Lourdes bowed to the bishop and kissed his ruby ring with the salutation "Your Eminence" while Martin gazed at the gold crucifix around his neck.

"Please have a seat. My condolence on your father's passing," the bishop offered sincerely. Looking at Lourdes he asked,

"How long has it been?"

"Almost two months. It's hard to get used to…not so much that he is not home, but that he is not coming back," Lourdes said reflectively as her blue eyes moistened. Then with firmness she continued,

"Bishop, we are taking it well, ahh, as well as can be expected, but Martin seems depressed."

"What behaviors make you think he is upset?"

Martin listened as the bishop and his mother talked about him as though he were not even in the room. Then, looking at Martin, the bishop said,

"Sometimes people are mad at God. That is okay. God can take it, but can you?"

After a pause Martin responded with a soft and clear voice,

"Why did God take my dad away from me?"

The bishop loved the question *why*. So many people approached him just wanting to receive a yes or a no answer that did not admit of any nuance or subtlety, as if not to trouble him by having to give an explanation. Unfortunately, over time, the bishop reciprocated and his responses became shorter, his arguments made with the expediency of authority.

"How marvelous," the bishop thought to himself. "Here is this boy asking *why*, a question that reaches for the horizon of truth, the splendor of the mind. *Why*, a question that seeks love, the beauty of the soul; a question that echoes with the beauty of goodness in the sanctuary of conscience."

"It's God's will," Lourdes said as if to reprimand the question.

"Yes, it is God's will, and no it is not," the bishop said.

"God didn't create death. God rejoices in the living. For the first time you are feeling the pain and separation of death. Sad it is, but God so loves us that he sends his own Son to save us from sin and death, to remove the sting of death and restore us to the fullness of life. Though we cannot see your dad now, in faith we know that he lives."

"But why him? Why us?" Martin asked.

40

"It is right to ask why, but, humbly, we accept living without the answer," the bishop replied with the quality of a man living on the shore of a vast ocean, aware of being on the fringe of mystery.

"Not even the tragedies of sin and death can frustrate God's loving plan. St. Paul tells us that death follows from sin, the misuse of human freedom. God's providence embraces human freedom without destroying it. We will only really discover God's plan, which alone makes sense of the world and everything in it, at its consummation. Now we walk by faith and surrender to his mysterious providence, not as victims of conflicting forces, but as his beloved children empowered with an important part to fulfill in the drama of salvation."

"But you blessed his boat! You blessed *Isabel*," Martin groaned as he turned to his mother's outstretched arms. The bishop sighed and waited for Martin to turn back to him. Then he asked,

"*Isabel* is your dad's boat?"

"Yes," Martin answered.

"That your dad asked for a blessing for his boat shows he is a man of faith," the bishop said with a smile and strength that expressed admiration for Miguel.

"Through blessings, the church calls us to praise God, implore his protection, and provides us with ways of praying to restrain the power of evil in this world. When the church invokes God's blessing on an object, like your dad's boat, it is always with a view to the people who use the objects. When we blessed *Isabel* we placed everything that happens in and to the people in that boat under the umbrella of God's blessing. Even the dangers and difficulties, the joys and sorrows are placed under God's blessing. Thus, even your father's death, in a mysterious way, though painful, can be a sanctifying event for him and the community."

Martin, a little confused, nodded anyway. The bishop stood up saying,

"I'd like you to meet someone."

Lourdes and Martin followed the bishop out of his office along a corridor and down another stairway. They entered the sacristy of the cathedral and then emerged into the sanctuary. They walked along a side aisle all the way down the nave of the nineteenth century church.

The bishop stopped in front of an image of Mary's most chaste spouse, Joseph, holding Jesus as a boy. The bishop always referred members of households without a father, due to death or divorce, to Saint Joseph.

"Martin, I know no one can take your dad's place, but just as Saint Joseph was the foster father to Jesus, so he can be to you. Contemplate this image and ask for his help."

Martin nodded. Then the bishop said a prayer invoking the protection of St. Joseph and the consolation of the Holy Spirit. He shared a sign of peace with Martin and Lourdes and gave them his blessing.

"See you Sunday," the bishop said as he left.

Lourdes and Martin walked out of the cathedral onto the city's main square, a garden of green plants and high palms with a large circular gazebo at the center. Lourdes bought Martin some carrot juice. Together, they sat on a bench and watched as the city prepared for the Carnival.

Ash Wednesday, the day that marks the beginning of forty days of collective purification set between earthly glamour and heavenly glory, between the Carnival and The Easter Triduum, was only a few weeks away.

Lourdes and Martin returned from the city square to a home covered with vibrant feathers, sparkling beads and colorful cloth. The sewing machine hummed in busy anticipation of the

Carnival. Martin' sisters stitched cotton, satin, taffeta and chiffon into a myriad of costumes.

Martin used to play in the cloth at home and hide in the fabric's folds in the stores. Now, only a few days after the visit with the bishop, Martin resumed his passive moping around the house and actively antagonized his sisters.

Trust and fear battled to a stalemate within Martin. Adjusting to life without his dad frustrated him. Martin started covering up his feelings like an oyster overlaying an irritant with calcium carbonate to form a hard pearl. Irrational thoughts, hidden from his awareness, assailed the recesses of Martin's heart.

"If I had been with my dad in *Isabel*, he would still be here. If I had swum out to save him and not gone for help, he would still be here."

It didn't matter that Miguel did not allow his nine-year-old son to go with him at night and that he was not yet capable of swimming two miles.

Finally, Lourdes called Benjamin to take Martin out for the day so the sewing, an important source of income for the family, could continue unimpeded. She also thought a visit with his uncle would help Martin.

Benjamin and Martin took a bus to the *Olas Atlas* seaside promenade and got off at a fountain called *Continuidad de Vida*. A young man and woman embrace as they look into the future, drawn with the joyful confidence of a playful pod of dolphins leaping forward out to sea. Close by, just a short walk away, was the place Martin had spotted *Isabel*. Benjamin chose the place on purpose.

"The continuity of life. What does that mean to you?" Martin thought for a moment and looked into his uncle's eyes.

"I guess it just means that life goes on."

"Yes, you're right, life goes on." The silence that followed gave the sound of the salt water waves a chance to heal Martin's noiseless wounds.

"Martin, I have another meaning for you. I see your dad in you. In a way, his life continues through yours, from generation to generation." Benjamin gave Martin a pat on the back as they began walking along the smooth seaside promenade set above the rocky coves. Rounding a point guarded by a rusty cannon, Benjamin pointed to a near-shore reef.

"During high swells the surfers arrive here with their boards. They call it *Canones*. I've seen some surfers ride a wave for more than a kilometer."

Today the waves at *Los Pinos* Beach were flat. Two sets of footprints, side-by-side, moved over the sand. Benjamin and Martin sat down on the warm shore and looked to the brown islands over a blue sea. The balm of his uncle's love and the heat of the sun had softened Martin. He began to cry and Benjamin let him. After the tears began to dry, Martin felt a little embarrassed. He covered himself with bravado saying,

"One day I'll swim to those islands from here."

"I think you might one day. Let's have a start now." They removed their clothes and splashed in the warm water. Martin already knew how to swim but he had never been out so far, having followed in the wake of his uncle well past the reef and into the bay. He didn't feel timid but powerful as the tear drops diluted quickly in the ocean.

Soon, Benjamin and Martin began swimming once a week. Not long afterward, Martin stroked through the soothing seas every day. He could break the surface in anger and it would still gently hold him. He could dive in and the ocean would hide him. He could exhaust himself kicking against it on the way out and it would use its energy to push his tired body back in.

Martin stayed in school and excelled. When he graduated, Mazatlán offered many job opportunities in fishing and tourism. Martin decided to work on the shrimp boats and fished from *Isabel* like his father before him. He swam every day, even in the early summer, before the rains came. He didn't mind the burning *quemaduras*, the bluish purple tentacles of the small jellyfish, that clung to him. He felt that, somehow, he deserved to suffer.

By July, the thunder storms struck and the streets of Mazatlán became rivers that flowed into the ocean. The flashes of lightning and the pounding of thunder shook the sky and put the fear of God into every mortal being. The burning jellyfish were washed away, but the sting of Miguel's death would not leave Martin, so Martin decided to leave Mazatlán.

Lourdes begged Martin to go to church with her before his departure. He had stopped celebrating years before. He couldn't resist his mother's pleas so he went with her to the cathedral. During the Communion Procession the people sang *Pescador de Hombres*. The words, "I will seek other shores," seemed to confirm Martin's decision.

Lourdes asked her son to continue going to church and to write. All Martin could manage after he reached Los Angeles was sporadic prayer at night, before bed, and an occasional phone call to his mother in Mexico.

Chapter Eight
Ten Years to San Pedro

Martin, ten years removed from his father's death and a thousand miles from home, emerged from the Pacific next to the ocean side of the San Pedro breakwater. He turned back and surveyed the path of the day's swim with some satisfaction. His eyes changed from grey to blue and back to grey as they passed over the shallows and scanned the depths.

"The distance is still not far enough but better than yesterday," Martin thought to himself. "Soon, I'll swim to Angel's Gate and back."

Angel's Gate, the name given to the lighthouse at the end of the breakwater, marked the entrance to the Port of Los Angeles. When Martin entered the port for the first time six months before, he could not see the rotating green light but could hear the two note blast of the foghorn. He had been a stowaway on a ship carrying a cargo of canned shrimp from Mazatlán.

"It almost feels like home," Martin said to himself as he felt the sand under his feet and the warm saltwater drying on his browned 5'9" frame. He walked from the sand to the Cabrillo Beach Bath House and informally confirmed the number *77* written after the words *water temperature.*

The sea temperature off the Southern California coast registered ten degrees above average. The 1998 *El Nino* current that brought the warm water had been foretold, granting many of the fishermen Martin now worked for the chance to outfit their boats for tuna.

The run of tuna in the coastal waters off San Pedro left some of the locals dreaming of reopening the cannery on Terminal Island. Martin, for his part, shared the joy and hope of the fishing community magnified as it was by millennial anticipation and the vigor of his nineteen years.

Departing the bath house, Martin walked to a bus stop and waited, pondering his plans for the future. He still felt he had a chance to become a member of the crew on one of the fishing boats at Port 73: even though he knew that the Italian and Croatian immigrants who owned and operated the vessels had large families and numerous relatives for hire. Before Martin began processing his contingency plans, the bus arrived. The door opened and the driver greeted Martin,

"How was the swim today?"

"The warm water makes me faster," Martin replied as he took a seat on a molded plastic chair. The bus accelerated away from the bath house, turned on 22nd Street and went north on Harbor Boulevard. Martin watched as the bus overtook a trolley car that reminded him of the open air *pulmonias* on the streets of Mazatlán. Moving majestically down the Main Channel in the opposite direction was a cruise ship.

The bus left the waterfront at Fifth Street and skirted Old Town San Pedro. The bus driver stopped, knowing Martin's destination on the fringes of town, without a ring of the bell or a pull of the cord.

Walking a couple of blocks, Martin arrived at a small one bedroom apartment he shared with two other men. It was half-past four in the afternoon but Jose and Antonio had just awakened. Already laughing, Jose asked about Martin's swim as Antonio, one of the biggest and strongest men working the docks, drank coffee from a cup he held at the bottom, the handle of the mug too small to accommodate any of his large fingers.

"The water is warm. Why not join me tomorrow?" Martin invited.

"Oh, no," Jose responded with a nervous laugh. "I'm not swimming with the sharks. Thanks anyway," he said as he shook his head and laughed again.

"If you're not going for a swim, why not take a shower," Antonio brooded over his coffee, thinking Jose's body odor spoiled the aroma of the percolated brew.

"That's okay. I'm not dirty," Jose said with nervous laughter. Martin shrugged, looking at Antonio, who due to the small size of the apartment always thought Jose smelled.

"Martin, don't you think Antonio should pay more rent than us?" Jose asked.

"Why?"

"Because he takes up so much more space," Jose said, pleased with himself for the joke and laughing hysterically while darting away from Antonio's grasp like a fish in a barrel.

Later, after dinner and a game of dominoes, Martin, Antonio and Jose boarded the bus to Fishermen's Wharf. They walked in the moist night air to Port 73. Antonio took a pair of worn gloves from his back pocket; Jose started talking to some of the other night-laborers and Martin studied the container used to raise the tuna from the boats to the platform adjacent to the Municipal Fish Market.

Everyone on or near the platform was ready to greet the fishing boats as they returned from short nocturnal rounds or multi-week voyages. While Martin, Antonio and Jose's waiting was tinged with weariness, their muscles taut just thinking of the impending toil, the brokers, who bought and sold the fish, anticipated profits for supplying the demand of sushi markets and restaurants.

48

The boats themselves incorporated all the elements of the eons used for catching the sea prey: wood hulls with iron implements and the volley of sonar. As the boats approached, Martin could see the lights and the ladders, then the cranes and the cables, the pulleys, ropes and winches. The mound of black net sparkled like sequins, the scales of mighty fish caught in the mesh and now iced in the hold.

"Who's first?" Antonio asked.

"*Endurance*," Martin replied.

As the boat drew closer, the captain hailed for assistance. After the bow and stern lines were secured and the *Endurance* was parallel to the dock, Martin, Antonio and Jose went down a ladder, walked along the deck and found their way to the hold of the boat. Antonio reached for the bucket lowered down by an employee of the Municipal Fish Market to keep it from swinging. Then he, Martin and Jose began to load the bluefin tuna and yellowtail into the bucket. The container was raised and lowered four more times until the hold of the *Endurance* was empty.

Around midnight, and after Martin, Antonio and Jose had filled the bucket with fish fifteen times from three different holds, Martin studied the floating queue of boats waiting to off-load their cargo. Then he exclaimed,

"It's the *Saint Augustine*."

The captain maneuvered his craft to the dock, came down from the pilot house and greeted the men in Spanish.

"*Hola*, Luigi," Jose responded. "How's the catch?"

"It'll keep you land lovers occupied and would pay off my debts if not for the forty thieves up there," Luigi responded so as to be heard by the buyers who gave the price for the fish, presumably set by the market, and determined the weight. None of the buyers, however, took offense. The year was the most profitable in fifteen.

When the hold of the *St. Augustine* had given up most of the catch, Luigi poured some hot coffee.

"Thanks," Antonio said, "I need a rest."

Luigi, pulling on a lock of his grey beard, responded by quoting the saint, known as the doctor of grace, for whom his boat was named.

"You have made us for yourself, and our hearts are restless until they rest in you." Then Luigi, reminiscing, said,

"This voyage is like the nights we had when I was a boy forty years ago. We would only off-load the *top of the hatch* fish here, the quality tuna that was most fresh and least bruised. Then dad would turn the rudder toward Terminal Island. That is where the rest of the tuna was cleaned, baked and canned. We thought those nights would last forever." Luigi sighed and took a sip of his coffee. The pace of the men off-loading the fish slowed as they listened.

"Back then," Luigi continued, "we praised the saints – all the boats were named for one. Then, after so many lousy years, the owners started to sell and captains changed the names of their boats from the saints that had abandoned them to names like persistence and survivor."

"Saint Augustine is coming through for you this year," Martin said.

"Yes, but this year is a time of consolation after a long torment. We have the *El Nino* to thank. But by this time next year… That's why we'll go to Mexico," Luigi said, stroking his boat tenderly and then patting it confidently.

"Is that why you have been learning Spanish?" Jose asked.

"Yes," Luigi said with a wink and a pull of his beard. "As Saint Augustine says, 'What man wants trouble and hardship? He commands that they be endured, not that they be liked.'" Luigi looked up to heaven, smiled, sighed, and continued, "'No man likes what he endures, although he likes to endure it. Woe to the adversities of this world, for they can make a wreck of endurance!'"

Luigi briefly rubbed the shoulders of Jose and then shook the hands of the night-laborers. He paid Martin generously and yelled as he returned to the pilot house,

"I hope to see you here two or three nights from now with another belly-load full of fish. If I'm late...," Luigi trailed off, gently turned down his roughly bearded face, remembering another quote from Saint Augustine, and said in a gruff voice, "Late have I loved you, O Beauty so ancient and so new, too late have I loved you! You were with me but I was not with you."

Chapter Nine
A Meeting at the Bus Stop

"May I take your order?" Israel asked, the green hazel of his eyes set against his white shirt, the black of his hair shinning like oil. The couple asked Israel about the special again, made a decision, and changed their minds.

"Don't worry," Israel responded to the apologetic patrons. "It is good that you take such care in your selection." After five years at the finest restaurant in San Pedro, Israel knew the next question the couple would ask and provided an answer.

"What do you suggest?"

"I recommend the fresh swordfish or the Prime Rib cooked to perfection. You'll want a bottle of Pinot Noir with the fish or a robust Merlot with the steak."

Israel started waiting tables in Guadalajara after he left the home where his brother was killed by Orlando Melendez in *Los Altos de Jalisco*. Working his way north, Israel met a family in Puerto Escondido that took him across the border at Tijuana in their motor-home. Upon arriving in the United States, Israel chose to live in San Pedro because he had relatives in town. The city was also named for the patron saint of Hernan Cortés, the Spanish conquistador of Mexico.

Israel still had the biography of Cortés given to him by his dad but did not follow his father's advice about continuing his education at the University. Instead, Israel honed his English by mimicking those he served at the restaurant and listening attentively to the conversation of self-important persons who wanted to be heard. He visited the San Pedro branch of the Los Angeles City Library every day it was open and studied the culture, trends and industry gleaned from the previous night's patrons.

At twenty-five years of age, Israel was not only well informed, tall, dark, and handsome but exuded a machismo that men admired and women either covertly adored or overtly abhorred. Israel attributed his intensity and will to dominate to Catalonian testosterone and masked it with an easygoing attitude. When memories of his brother's shooting impinged upon him, the powerlessness he felt motivated him to redouble his efforts at making money.

In addition to his pay and tips, Israel also rented two apartments, subletting space in each. Having just made arrangements for a third property, one in which he would live, Israel looked for someone to whom he could rent the other room. Israel had developed a financial acumen and ability to strike deals that earned him a reputation at the restaurant.

Israel served the couple swordfish and Prime Rib. The Pinot Noir had already been opened by the wine steward and stood proudly in an ice bucket. Israel was approaching another table when the restaurant manager took him aside and asked, in a rapid tempo like that found in the busy kitchen,

"I'd like you to go to Fishermen's Wharf in the morning and order this for tomorrow night." The manager handed a piece of paper to Israel. "Have them deliver it in the early afternoon."

"Okay," Israel responded, having run purchasing errands on many occasions.

The next morning Israel exited the bus near the Municipal Fish Market just before sunrise. He walked along the loading dock where men busily moved wax boxes filled with fish into truck trailers. He stepped over puddles in his leather boots and tipped his cowboy hat to those he met as he wove his way along the platform. He entered one of the stalls and watched men with sharp knives fillet fish while others, clad in yellow slickers, stirred an ice bath with long wooden paddles. A man with a knife, noticing Israel's boots and hat, turned from his bloody task and said with a John Wayne accent,

"Pilgrim, you just take it easy and throw them guns over there in that creek."

Israel, resembling a cowboy, was as out of place among the fishermen as a rodeo in Fiji.

"Hey, partner, the Duke told me to tell you he passed through last night. When he left, he went that way," the burly man said, pointing his knife emphatically at the door.

Glancing at an elevated office, Israel saw the seller he had come to speak to about a quote. The fish merchant hung up the phone and acknowledged Israel. Slowly, Israel raised his right hand, thumb up, index finger pointed out toward the man with the knife, and the remainder of the fingers curled in so that it took the form of a pistol. Then he twice made the clicking sound from the side of his mouth that tells a horse it's time to move on.

"Howdy, pilgrim. Time to saddle up and go west," Israel said to the stunned man who angrily waved his cutlery. The seller arrived and the man went back to his carving as Israel and the merchant conducted their business.

After making arrangements for delivery, Israel departed the stall at the Municipal Fish Market. Approaching the bus stop,

54

he saw three Mexicans with matted hair and soiled clothes sitting on a bench.

Martin, Antonio and Jose sat quietly at the bus stop as the seagulls squawked and swooped around the last of the returning tuna boats in the distance. The bus bound for Old Town San Pedro halted, the door sprung open, the passengers boarded, deposited their coins and sat down.

"You men off-load the boats?" Israel asked over the rumble of the bus' accelerating motor and cranking gears. Martin nodded affirmatively as Antonio grunted and Jose snoozed.

"You're on your way home after a long night," Israel said with a note of understanding that struck a chord with Martin.

"Yes. We worked through the night. The boats kept coming, one after another."

The bus turned from the water and climbed Fifth Street.

"I suppose the work wouldn't be so tough if you had a decent place to return home to." Israel paused and then asked, "Where do you live?"

"We share an apartment on Sepulveda," Martin answered.

"What's it like?"

"Small."

"I just moved into a place on Cabrillo. I have an extra large room for rent. Why not take a look? It's on the way."

"Thank you, but right now we just want a hot meal and a long sleep," Martin replied.

"How about I show you the place. It will just take a minute. It's one block from the next stop. Then I'll buy you all breakfast," Israel persisted.

Antonio, who had been listening indifferently, lifted his head. Martin noted his roommate's interest and said,

"Okay. My name is Martin. That is Antonio and he's Jose."

"I am Israel."

By the first of the following month, Israel's new tenants moved into his apartment. Soon they all became friends. The group gathered each day before Israel left for work. On one such afternoon Israel said,

"The *migra* are on the hunt at the restaurant lately." Israel referred to agents of the Immigration and Naturalization Department. "The manager let me know. He apologized and said that I might need to take a job in the kitchen, out of sight. I won't do it. I'll find another place to work."

"Some say they're putting pressure on all the restaurants now. It is an election year in California," Martin observed.

"What do you care? You can't vote," Antonio said with some aggravation. "I've had my green-card for a year now. I can't even apply for a job as a longshoreman until I become a citizen."

"We just have to be patient and keep trying," Martin insisted, sensitive to the current affairs because they affected his efforts to secure new employment. Unbeknown to his roommates, each day en route to his swim, Martin paced the property of the Municipal Fish Market in the hopes of landing a job. He wanted to be the one to raise and lower the bucket down to the boats, not one of the men who filled the container.

A week later Martin's persistence paid off and he was hired. But not before Israel quit the restaurant where he had worked the previous five years. To add insult to injury, no restaurant would hire Israel as a waiter despite his recommendations.

On the day before beginning his new job, Martin went for his daily swim. He still hadn't informed his friends about his new position and hoped a tactic for doing so would emerge after his strokes and kicks through the choppy waters. After his swim,

Martin, still unsure about how to share his good news, returned to the apartment he rented from Israel.

Israel, who worked since his eighth birthday on the farm in *Jalisco*, provided Martin with the opportunity he sought. Israel, excruciatingly frustrated by his current unemployment, stood above Antonio and Jose and said,

"I might have to raise the rent."

"Well, then, it is a good thing I was just hired by the market as the crane operator for the bucket."

Antonio, who was standing up to meet Israel's threat with his intimidating bulk, turned toward Martin as the apartment thickened with a dumbfounded hush. Then, slowly, Martin's roommates uttered half-hearted congratulations, coveting the job themselves. Martin sensed the initial reaction of his friends to the news as polite envy. Martin, understanding the reaction, countered,

"Let's go to Raul's Place tonight. I'm buying"

The face of Jose turned from a pout to a smile as he cheered with a wide grin. Antonio smiled too, warning,

"Just make sure you don't dump the bucket on us," as he embraced his friend and glared at Israel, who remained obstinate.

"I can't wear this shirt for another day! I need a new one if I am going out with you tonight."

Israel, Antonio, Jose and Martin all entered Raul's Place that Saturday night with new shirts, pants and shoes. Martin nervously reproached himself for spending the money he had planned on sending to his mother in Mazatlán. But, as they walked through the restaurant together, he knew he and his friends looked good.

Chapter Ten
Love Blossoms

Vanessa, or Violet as she was known to the patrons, watched Martin and his friends enter her father's restaurant as she danced the *Folklorico*. Vanessa's primeval scent for success rested on Martin and their eyes met.

"This way," Raul said, leading Martin, Israel, Jose and Antonio to a table with a view of the stage. Once seated, the men watched, mesmerized, as the girls' dresses swirled in colors as red as a matador's muleta, in yellows as bright as the sun, in deep lavender and pinks only matched by the lipstick painted on their voluptuous lips and the feathers of a flamingo. Yet the ladies, rolling with rhythm, maintained a certain modesty as their faces stayed calm, their eyes somehow distant. The dancers' black buckled shoes seemed to be so attuned to the rhythmic strings of the guitar, it was as if their feet moved along a nylon tightrope and the leaps and landings kept those watching in the same suspense.

Israel grabbed at Raul's shirt sleeve and said excitedly,

"Wow! Where did you get those girls?" Raul responded with a firm yet reasonable voice,

"The one on the left is Rose. Her mom, my wife, gave birth to her nineteen years ago. Then there are her sisters: Violet,

Daisy and my daughter Tulip. Enjoy their beauty, but don't pick
the flowers!"

Raul left the table after taking an order for a round of
tequila. The friends laughed at Israel's blunder and continued to
watch the girls, who danced like flowers swaying in the wind.
Israel, who noticed Martin's special interest in Vanessa, taunted
him saying,

"I think Martin has found a flower but he has no vase to
place it in," reminding Martin that he was poor and without a
home.

"Which one?" Jose and Antonio asked.

"Violet, the girl second from the left."

Vanessa had just turned seventeen and was not the
prettiest of her sisters but carried a little more weight in all the
right places. Her black straight hair was braided intricately along
both sides of her head, coming together as it reached down her
swayed back.

Martin denied Israel's observation but returned to Raul's
Place each of the following nights and inched his way, one table
at a time, closer to the stage. The second night Sara, Vanessa's
older sister, said,

"I think that guy is watching you." Vanessa deftly
replied,

"You think so?" On the third night Sara said,

"We all think that funny-looking guy with the big ears
likes you." Vanessa, upset at the comment, huffed,

"What, him, he's not funny-looking," in a voice that gave
herself away and left the girls giggling.

After two weeks, Martin's designs were obvious to
everyone including Vanessa's father. Martin didn't know
whether to ask for permission to date his daughter or to speak to
Vanessa herself. Finally, Vanessa helped the sluggish romance

along by feigning a fall. Martin was so close to the stage by this time that Vanessa practically somersaulted into his lap.

Martin reached under Vanessa's arms to pull her up.

"Are you okay?"

"Yes," Vanessa replied, actually a bit shaken from the stunt. Martin backed away as Raul approached and the hysterics of Vanessa's sisters settled down. Raul thanked Martin for helping his daughter and invited him to sit with the family. Vanessa and Martin looked at each other again, and this time everyone noticed.

In the evenings to follow, Vanessa sat alone with Martin during her breaks from dancing. Once she caught her breath she spoke of what she was learning as a part-time student of Chicano Studies at a community college. Vanessa, an Hispanic, born in the United States, knew more about Mexico than Martin. One evening's conversation brought a blush to Vanessa's cheeks.

"My teacher showed us a picture of K'awil, and told me that I was now under the Mayan snake-footed god of lineage."

"Is that because you are so interested in your forefathers?"

"Yes," Vanessa answered.

"The only forefather of yours I am concerned about is your dad."

"Oh, he likes you," Vanessa reassured him.

"The only story about a snake I know of, except the one in the Bible," Martin added, "is one my uncle Benjamin told me. At a certain time of the year the snake enters a hole in the ground. When the snake comes back out, the earth blossoms." In the pause that followed, Vanessa's cheeks flushed as they laughed. Vanessa thought for a moment and then rejoined,

"The first great civilization in the Valley of Mexico had a female goddess associated with caves and a male deity that brought water." Vanessa spoke of *Teotihuacán* with its pyramid of the sun, moon and temple of the feathered serpent, as her gold and silver earrings, depicting the heavenly bodies, dangled seductively from her ear lobes and a crucifix guarded her chest.

Raul watched his daughter and Martin like a hawk and noticed that they were falling in love. Thirteen months after Martin and Vanessa clinched their infatuation with a kiss, they sealed their love by consummating their marriage. The wedding took place at Mary, Star of the Sea in San Pedro. The newlyweds went to Catalina Island for the honeymoon.

Soon after, the couple was pregnant with their first child whom they named Luke. Vanessa began praying like everything depended on God while Martin worked like everything depended on him. After Luke's birth, Martin was content to pay the rent, send money to his mother in Mazatlán, and feed his family. Raul was thinking about the education of his grandchildren. Martin had a cyclical view of time and Raul had a linear outlook.

One afternoon Martin and Vanessa entered the restaurant, placed Luke in a highchair, and talked about the day's somewhat monotonous but predictably comfortable events. Raul approached with an idea for the days to come. Raul baited Martin and Vanessa with the question,

"I am thinking of adding fish to the menu. What do you think?"

"What's wrong with beef and chicken?" Martin asked defensively, sick of the limp fins, laboriously loaded, he hauled up from the boats to the market with the crane.

"We have shrimp enchiladas and you just added pork chile verde," Vanessa added.

"We have some new customers who work in shipping," Raul pointed out. "They keep asking for fish and they are willing to pay for it."

"Oh, that reminds me," Martin raised his voice excitedly,

"Antonio just got a job as a longshoreman in Long Beach."

"How did he do that?" Vanessa inquired. "I didn't think they hired Hispanics. Didn't you say he is as strong as a horse? Yes, he is the one with those broad shoulders and thick legs."

"Well, I once told him how I got my job. And we all know there is less work right now, though I think the fish will come back soon," Martin said, taking some share in his friend's success. "Anyway, he got the job. Maybe it is because he is an oversized mule," Martin said as if to remind his wife of the aesthetics of his own slender body.

Martin and Vanessa, having diverged so far from Raul's original question, heard it again:

"What about adding fish to the menu?"

"Well, there is still plenty of quality fish but many of the boats are being refitted for sardines. They catch these little fish, no bigger than my hand, and send them to China or make fertilizer out of them. The Italians love'em," Martin said as he held up his calloused palms.

"Just the same, come by when you are off work next week. Use my truck and I'll give you some money to buy ten pounds of yellowtail and a few pounds of whatever else looks good," Raul directed.

"A week. You don't even have a recipe yet, do you?" Vanessa asked.

"Martin will get the recipe from his mom in Mazatlán and you can change the menus," Raul responded rapidly, as if anticipating the question.

"Okay, dad," Vanessa said happily, knowing that the task could be done at home and just in time to help pay the rent. Her expression turned to a frown, however, when Martin asked,

"Is Israel going to be back next week?"

"Yes," answered Raul.

Israel, at Martin's urging, was hired as a waiter at Raul's Place. It bothered Vanessa that Martin practically begged her dad on behalf of his friend. She worked hard to build up familial good will and to have it dissipated outside her home was more discomforting than a leak in the bathtub. What made it all the worse was that her dad, who had always required everyone, including herself and her sisters, to bus tables before becoming a waiter or waitress at his restaurant, broke what was to her something akin to a commandment.

Martin's plea was made on the grounds that Israel was a proud man, older than he, and from a family with a large amount of land in Mexico. Vanessa agreed that Israel was proud, but her dad had always taught her that patience and humility receive lasting rewards. The meek shall inherit the land! And to top it all off, Martin had predicted that Israel would be tipped higher than anyone in a month's time because he knew how to speak to the customers. What did that comment say about her and her sisters?

Vanessa perceived the streak of craziness in Israel that made him utterly magnetic to men younger than he until it got them hurt or in trouble. Anytime she tried to caution Martin or suggest he not go out with Israel, the retort was that she was just sore because he was making such good tips. Indeed, Israel's risqué chatter tickled the customer's fancy as much as his recklessness scratched at Vanessa's intuition and ruffled her brooding feathers.

"Oh, he's coming back. How wonderful," Vanessa said sarcastically, the naturally acorn-shaped bridge of her noble Mayan nose protruding farther, her black eyes even darker. "He is only here for a couple of months and he is already taking what will probably be the first of many vacations!" Vanessa turned and left. Martin and Raul hunched their shoulders as if to say,

"What did we do?"

The following week Martin stopped by Raul's Place to pick up the truck and purchase the fish. He fumbled with his new wallet, the only contents being an equally new California driver's license. Raul met him in the parking lot and handed him the keys and some money.

Martin felt a sense of confidence for the trust Raul placed in him, as well as an excitement akin to that of a fifteen-year-old when he or she takes the car out for the first time. Martin, now just turned twenty-one years old, listened impatiently as Raul talked about the idiosyncrasies of the truck. Finally, Raul took his hand off the side view mirror he had been holding and Martin drove away toward Port 73.

A few hours later, the blue truck returned with the fish, coughing its way back up Fifth Street, not because of the load, but because it was old. When Martin turned into the parking space behind Raul's Place he saw Israel and honked the horn to the tune of *La Cucaracha*. Israel greeted Martin by thrusting his arm through the open window and grabbing Martin's forearm and shaking it as he joked,

"I go to Jalisco for a few days to kick cow paddies and you add fish fillets to the menu." Martin turned to shake his friend's hand. Israel went to meet it but then stopped, saying,

"I've got something for us to shake on." And taking a wry look at the two boxes in the bed of the truck, he asked,

"How much will you give me if we sell all this fish tonight?" Martin thought for a moment. Then a smile crossed his face as he looked with circumspection at Israel and asked,

"What arrangement have you made with Raul?" Israel laughed and shook his friend's hand.

In a few months fish became a hot item on the menu at Raul's Place. In addition, Martin made daily deliveries to three other Mexican restaurants. Yet a problem began to surface. Some days, no fish could be purchased at the port.

Martin sat sulking across the table from Raul on a morning the boats had returned without a catch. Raul had a newspaper opened in front of him and read the headline article to Martin.

"Where Are the Fish? Are They Coming Back? The consensus is the ocean off California has run dry from the ravages of pollution and the plunder of over fishing. At a time when the once abundant, open-water game has become scarce, restaurants in coastal cities from San Diego to San Francisco, and desert metropolises such as Las Vegas and Phoenix, are teeming with people with a hunger for fish."

Raul checked Martin's face for a reaction as he peered up from the newspaper. Martin continued to sulk, masking his frustration as he regressed into thinking to himself,

"If my dad were here, he would catch the fish we need."

"Can you take the truck tomorrow after work and buy some marigolds?" Vanessa asked, interrupting Martin's thoughts as she stood above him at the table with an apron on. "Remember, we are setting up for the Day of the Dead. I even have a college friend visiting. You remember Claudia?"

"Yes," Martin responded ambivalently as he looked at Raul with feelings of unworthiness. Raul, sensing his son-in-law's mood, said,

"There's nothing you can do to make the fish return. Relax." Raul patted Martin on the back as he stood up and walked over to the playpen where Luke slept.

Chapter Eleven
Marigolds

The following night an orange harvest moon, hanging low in the sky, filled the frames of the southwest-facing windows at Raul's Place. A cozy bunch of marigolds lay carefully on the creaky, wooden floor near the stage, now the resting place for a few skulls, some paper skeletons and pieces of lumber.

The last of the patrons, whose faces flickered with the golden light of a candle, sipped hot coffee and shared a creamy flan. Martin placed Luke in a highchair next to the banquet table. Bea and Laura, Vanessa's two younger sisters, just finished filling the water glasses when Antonio and Jose arrived. Raul welcomed his guests with some smooth tequila to warm them on a chapping, cool autumn night.

Martin, Jose and Antonio greeted one another with easy laughter and firm embraces.

"Hey, *Tonto. Hombre*," they said to each other.

Vanessa arrived with her black hair in a braid, giving her the beautiful vulnerability of a peasant girl. But all Martin's friends knew such a look was deceiving in Vanessa.

"Before you guys get too comfortable, how about putting the altar together. There is still time before dinner is served and it will give you an appetite."

"Oh, that's okay," Jose said, "I'm already hungry." A pause ensued and Jose started to laugh slowly in a high pitched nervous way that only sped up and became louder as he looked at each person for approval. Vanessa placed her hands on her hips, pointed to the lumber on the stage and then motioned for her sisters to follow her back to the kitchen.

Meanwhile, Israel, who had been serving the last of the patrons, changed into his cowboy boots and ambled over to the others. He looked at his friends through hazel eyes to receive their accolades before sitting down ceremoniously. Then, in jest, and with a voice full of authority, he started giving directions on how the altar should be built and positioned.

"If you keep that up, we're going to make sure you are the first sacrifice offered on this altar," Martin said. The banter continued as a scheme took shape for removing Israel from his chair. Israel heard the whispering and decided to play along with his friends.

Jose and Martin approached Israel, as though to talk to him, and then picked up the back of his chair. With Antonio in front and the others in back, they strained to lift Israel upon their shoulders for a procession around the restaurant. Israel, unbalanced, toppled to the ground before he could ascend his throne.

The four friends, sprawled out on the floor in the middle of the room, laughed hysterically. Just then, a woman dressed like a cat entered. She wore black stockings that clung to her long legs. Pointed ears perked up from her pretty blond head and whiskers spread over her rosy cheeks. Vanessa followed as if trying to catch up. The laughter stopped. Martin sobered instantly, recognizing the woman as Vanessa's college friend. Jose and Israel looked at each other, then back at the woman, and jumped up with agile smiles to meet the feline. Antonio, who liked Vanessa's sister Sara, arose more slowly.

Claudia stood awkwardly in her costume, as if a joke had been told and she didn't understand the punch line. After a few seconds she asked herself, "Is the joke on me?" Vanessa rushed to Claudia's aid and whisked her away. The moment they left the room, the men looked at each other, and, with sides already aching, laughed again.

All the guests arrived by ten o'clock and took their seats at the table. Vanessa and Claudia wore *Folklorico* dresses. The black paint was wiped from Claudia's delicate nose but she kept fiddling with the borrowed dress, feeling discomfort mixed with lingering embarrassment.

Raul poured the wine and then called down God's blessing on some steaming soup that swirled upward. Jose watched Claudia take a drink of chardonnay and said,

"Don't worry about the costume from earlier. Just look at the way Israel is dressed!" Then the nervous laughter escalated as Jose glimpsed at each person, as if to give them permission to laugh, which they did, with the exception of Israel, who looked like a cowboy even without his hat, as he fastened his string tie.

"I thought it was a Halloween party," Claudia said.

"It is a party, not just for the living but for the dead," Vanessa replied.

"Boo!" Jose shouted. Startled, Claudia jerked in her seat. Everyone else glared at Jose. Giggling nervously, Jose did not laugh this time. After Claudia regained her composure, Vanessa said,

"Halloween is scarier than the Day of the Dead, if you ask me. Halloween is about dressing up in ghoulish costumes to scare away the spirits of those who died in the previous year. These spirits haunt the land in search of people to possess so they can escape an unknown afterlife. On All Souls, or the Day of the Dead, the spirits of our beloved departed don't come back to possess us but return to visit us. We feel close to them and affirm our faith that for the dead, life is changed, not ended."

What are those bright orange flowers for?" Claudia asked, reaching for something cheerier.

"Oh, those," Vanessa answered, "yes, the marigolds. The Aztecs used them to guide loved ones home. The plant, itself an annual, completes its life cycle in one year, like the rotation of the earth around the sun. The Aztecs worshipped the sun."

Raul came by during the discussion to remove some dishes, placed a gentle hand on Vanessa's shoulder, and softly quoted the words of a psalm that he had made his own.

"In the morning our life springs up and flowers: by evening it withers and fades... Our span is seventy years or eighty for those who are strong...and most of these are emptiness and pain."

Vanessa squeezed her dad's hand and remembered her mother, Dolores, who died from breast cancer the year after Vanessa's *quinceñera*.

Crying, Luke awoke from his nap. He rolled over on a quilt in the middle of the floor. Before he could crawl an inch, many at the table reached out to hold him.

"We used to visit the cemetery and bring flowers to the grave of my grandparents when we lived near Veracruz on the Gulf Coast," Antonio said.

"I thought you were from Tijuana," Martin protested.

"My parents moved to Tijuana when I was eight. But before that we lived near San Lorenzo," Antonio replied in a low and deeply resounding voice more typical of northern Mexico.

"My parents trace their ancestry back three thousand years to the Olmecs, the mother culture of Mesoamerica," Antonio continued as he looked at Claudia and asked,

"You haven't heard of the humid rain forests or seen the giant stone heads that guard the ancient city? Some weigh as much as thirty tons, sculpted with jaguar claws."

Antonio, with skin as moist as oil and smooth as chocolate, embodied the riches of southern Mexico. Even his large head resting on a short neck resembled the colossal Olmec heads of the region, not only in size but also in features. Antonio's full lips moved under a broad nose as his eyes sparkled. He spoke of ball courts and pyramids.

Having finished dinner, Martin, Israel and Jose left the table to resume work on the altar. Claudia listened to Antonio but her attention kept returning to Israel as she peered over her wine glass at his back side. Vanessa observed her friend's body language, tapped her on the hand, and shook her head from side to side.

"Israel, tell us something about your family," Vanessa said from the end of the table closest to the stage. "I bet you can trace your royal Spanish blood back to, say, Don Quixote and his foolish chivalry. Or maybe you identify more with the wanton cavorting of Don Juan?"

Vanessa's comment received a round of laughter from everyone but Israel.

"Who is Don Juan?" Claudia asked innocently, wanting to learn more about Israel. Israel, not to lose an opportunity for self-aggrandizement, replied,

"It is true. I seek adventure as they did. Give me chivalry for a cause and pure desire for the sake of love!" Vanessa placed her hand on top of Claudia's, and, preempting any more musing from Israel, said,

"All you need to know is that the Don," she said with a wink, "had a bad habit of attracting girls to himself. Hapless maidens would give up a good match with another responsible man for no marriage at all with a man who would bring her nothing but momentary pleasure followed by sorrow and pain."

"Ah, but what a moment," Israel rejoined romantically as he glanced at Claudia, who looked down into her chardonnay. Then, sensing that he had gone too far, Israel deflected attention from himself, saying,

"If you want to hear something funny ask Jose how a chihuahua drove him from Mexico to the States." Before Jose could begin his story after a nervous laugh, Raul, Bea and Laura brought sweets for the altar.

Clearing his throat, Jose signaled his readiness to speak. Jose's dark black hair, cut short, moved with his sharp but friendly features. Standing near the altar but in front of the stage, his silver belt buckle shimmered with the word *Zacatecas*, his place of origin. He received the heirloom from his father for being the eldest of twelve children.

"My grandfather used to say, 'how rich we are to have this golden food' as he gnawed into a corn cob with a silver front tooth. 'We have gone from the wealth of silver to the poverty of gold, golden corn.' I grew up growing corn. I remember the smell of the burning husks after the harvest." Jose motioned over his shoulder and said,

"See that tamale Mr. Gonzalez brought to the stage?" Jose always called Raul Mr. Gonzalez out of respect. "The wrapping is a corn husk. The husk is a symbol of fertility. We might be poor, but we are full of life!"

"Did Jose mention that they also ferment pulque from the giant agaves to make liquid gold tequila in central Mexico?" Martin interjected. Suddenly laughing out loud, Jose moved to the table asking for a glass. Raul retrieved a bottle of tequila and poured a sip.

"To Zacatecas!" Martin exclaimed, leading the toast.

"The Aztecs would not allow able-bodied men under sixty to drink pulque," Vanessa added, as if to issue a warning with pointed levity. "If they were caught drinking once, they lost their hair; a second time, their home. If they did it a third time it would be the death of him and his whole family."

"And I thought California's three-strikes law was tough," Antonio said. Jose continued,

"I wasn't running from a chihuahua, I was running from the law. Here's what happened. I had a little sister. She needed an operation on her heart. We took her to the convent hospital, to the Franciscans. There was a doctor who visited there regularly. We couldn't afford the treatment but the doctor and the sisters did what they could to help her.

"I have this uncle. He sells corn, *elotes*, in Mexico City. I joined him to raise some money. I got a cart and started selling *elotes* too. We drenched them in butter, squirted lime and sprinkled red pepper all over them." Jose turned away with his eyes shut and his hand over his mouth in a reflex that is the prelude to a sneeze.

"I slept in the garage where my uncle kept our carts and corn. I returned home once a month with what I had earned to help pay for my sister's medicine. I also bought a radio that I kept with me all the time. Well, one day I was going up the hill with my cart, listening to music. I didn't hear the horn. I was listening to the music. When I saw the car, it was too late. I had to run my cart up onto the sidewalk. I almost ran over this old woman and her dog. She yelled at me, 'mal educado.' You see, in my family, work was more important than school. I'm not stupid; I just didn't finish school," Jose said defensively.

"But how would she know?"

As Jose paused, Vanessa looked over at Martin who was reaching for some sweet bread next to the altar.

"No, those are not for you," she said with a stern smile, "not yet, anyway."

"Who are they for?" Claudia asked.

"Remember how I told you the Day of the Dead is a party with the spirits of our loved ones who have passed on. You can say that they don't come back easily. They need to be enticed to return. That's why we place offerings of the person's favorite foods and drinks on the altar."

By this time, the altar had been covered. The adornments of orange marigolds, candles, skeletons, skulls and sweets were being placed. Next to the sweets, Raul poured Dolores' favorite drinks.

Raul and Dolores had lived in Morelia. Raul's wife had enjoyed the tropical fruit juices of the guyaba, lemon and jamaica. Raul was remembering their strolls through the plaza of St. Francis with its grand fountain and the words of the *Canticle of the Sun* about Sister Death.

"Dad, why are you pouring that now? We still have three more days."

"I'll just pour a few sips now and let you all have a taste of the rest," Raul replied absent-mindedly. Israel took a sip from a cup on the altar when Raul turned to Vanessa. Antonio caught him and warned,

"Don't take that now! Wait a few days."

"There might not be any left after the dead are done," Israel mooched with bravado.

Vanessa turned her attention back to Jose and asked,

"You didn't hit the dog or hurt the woman did you? Why the police?"

"Well," Jose said laughing nervously, "that was only our first meeting. It turns out she lived at the top of a hill. I had to climb this hill every day to get to my spot at the *Zócalo*. Every time I passed by she would pick up her chihuahua and hold it in her arms as if to protect it from me. Then she would yell, 'mal educado.' That upset me," Jose said with a tinge of anger in his voice.

"I knew some people on the hill so I asked them. Turns out she is rich. She even makes these clothes for her dog and feeds it beef every night. Well, turns out, she even took the dog to an animal doctor. The doctor did open heart surgery on the dog. Here I am with a poor sister who needs an operation and there she is with a dog that gets the operation."

"Rich bitch," Israel said with whimsical seriousness.

"The dog, I mean." Everyone chuckled but Jose, so intently did he retell the story. Changing pace and becoming more pensive, Jose continued,

"I guess I could have taken another street to the *Zócalo*, but I didn't. Part of me wanted to go by out of curiosity and blare my radio to get that little dog all riled up. Well, one day the dog came at me yapping and biting at my heels. I went to kick it away. The dog ran right into my foot. Then it started yelping and shaking. Then it died. The lady started yelling, 'You killed my dog, you killed my dog. I'm going to call the police,' she cried. The last thing I heard her say as I left with my cart of *elotes* was 'mal educado'."

"What did you do then?" Claudia asked, half appalled and on the edge of her seat.

"I just turned up my radio and went back down the street. I talked to my uncle. We decided I should go home. Then I came here looking for a way to make enough money to send some home."

"How is your sister?" Vanessa asked tentatively.

"She's fine. She had the operation. The sisters at the convent raised some money, plus what the family saved and we had enough. She was only eight then." Juan removed a frayed picture of his fourteen year old sister and passed it around.

74

"I guess you can say a chihuahua chased me to L.A."

"No, it was love for your sister that brought you here," Vanessa said.

"Do you ever get homesick?" Claudia asked.

"Yes, I miss the wide open spaces," Jose reflected, "the fields of gold corn, the green valleys."

Antonio heard Claudia's question as if it were directed to him and replied poetically,

"You haven't seen green until you visit the Yucatán Peninsula. You can watch vines of jade and emerald forests grow before your very eyes as smooth turquoise rivers flow nearby."

"I wish you could see the pyramid-shaped mountains reflected on mirrored lakes. And with the dramatic clouds..." Jose trailed off, lost in the beauty of his own imagination. His mind projected images from his travels from Zacatecas through Morelia to Mexico City.

"Everyone here thinks Mexico is warm and sunny. It is, at the seaside resorts. But there is a reason we are called the cloud people. Most towns are built up high, close to heaven, but ever so close to the earth."

Jose laughed nervously, and then looked around for approval. Many at the table were momentarily distant, the horizon of their minds cast back to the landscapes and seascapes of Mexico.

"If you want to understand Mexico, you need to meet the land and hear what it has to say to you in the silence," Antonio remarked.

"Quiet broken with the burst of musket shots; peace broken with fights over the land," Vanessa said with rankled emotion. Then she took a deep breath and continued speaking.

"After Cortés arrived in the sixteenth century and conquered the Aztecs, he rewarded his soldiers with land. By the nineteenth century the Indians didn't even have enough soil to plant corn. Then Emiliano Zapata led a revolt to recover the lands, whose titles dated from pre-Hispanic times. They called him the Centaur of the South for his horsemanship. He was shot to death, a martyr for the revolution."

"A martyr!" Israel objected. "He would not of had a horse if it weren't for the Spaniards! The Spanish Crown recognized the communal lands and actually created further grants. Yes, there were abuses under the *encomienda* system. The missionaries protested to the crown on behalf of the Indians. But it was the revolutionaries who outlawed the land held in common by the Indians and that of the church. What had been held in common was then turned into privately owned parcels. Most of the Indians had never owned land. In time they sold to the large landowners or *hacendados*. Later the Indians were reduced to hiring themselves out on these vast estates, land that had once been their own. That's what Zapata was fighting against. But don't blame the Spaniards!"

"Zapata, Zapatistas. I've heard that name before," Claudia said.

"Yes," Israel replied. "Many indigenous people seeking land or rights adopt his name and fight their own revolutions."

"There is a mural by Diego Rivera," Vanessa interjected, "the famous Mexican painter, showing Zapata bound in a blood red burial cloth, lying in an earthen cocoon close to the surface. Above him are mounds of earth from which grow stalks of corn. The roots of these plants branch downward like capillaries. There Zapata is, presumably dead, but to me he is always on the watch, with closed eyes; he is sleeping but ready to awaken should the Indian's corn above him be uprooted. For if it is, that same corn will feed a bloody revolution. I'm sorry Israel, but I think the name of the mural is *The Blood of the Revolutionary Martyrs Fertilizes the Earth*."

"I don't care what Rivera called it!" Israel roared as he stood up in his chair. "They were not martyrs, and he was a Communist. Diego Rivera paints an idealistic picture of what Mexico was like before the *conquista*, as if it were some kind of Garden of Eden. That it was not!"

Raul, seeing the escalation of voluminous words and rising tensions tried to calm things down with an observation, spoken gently,

"Claudia, we can disagree with Diego Rivera's interpretation of the past and his ideas about the future but, as an artist, his work expresses Mexico best."

"With respect, he is no martyr." Israel sat down but continued talking. "At the same time he was painting his mural, real martyrs were being made at the hands of the secular revolutionaries. They made stables of our churches, closed our schools, hunted down our priests and forbade the celebration of the Holy Sacraments. My family is from a ranch in Jalisco. We hid the priests in caves in the mountains of our land and my relatives fought and died to keep our churches open and teach our children the faith."

"Viva Cristo Rey!" Raul exclaimed.

"Viva Cristo Rey!" his family and guests cried back.

Raul said a prayer of thanks, dismissed everyone from the table and encouraged them to finish decorating the altar.

After the prayer, but before anyone could get up, Jose, laughing nervously and looking for Vanessa's approval as he chimed his glass with a fork, said,

"I have an announcement to make."

"Friends, we have talked about land and sacrifice. What does a man with a frontier spirit do when all the land has been discovered and settled? He moves to the sea. I was hired on for crew on the *Saint Augustine*. They are moving to Ensenada and I guess they can use my help down south. We leave at the beginning of next year."

Martin, Antonio and Israel looked at each other and then back at Jose. Raising his glass, Martin offered another toast,

"To a miner, a farmer and a friend, may you find what you seek and get rich doing it!" Then the men gathered around Jose and asked him questions. They recognized the *St. Augustine* as the finest boat at Port 73 for consistently having an unrivaled catch.

"If the *Augustine* is going south, other boats are going to follow. Is the fishing that good there?" Martin didn't want to state the evident corollary, "Is the fishing that lousy here?"

"If the fishing is good, I'm driving the truck there to meet you when you arrive with a belly full of fish!" Martin said half seriously but with full spontaneity.

"The truck has been empty too many days lately. If we drive down to Ensenada, we would have the fish we need and get a higher price for it here," Israel concurred.

"I did just get my license," Martin said eagerly.

"How are you going to keep the fish fresh?" Antonio asked.

"We would have to travel fast and keep the fish cold," Martin replied.

"They sell refrigerated trailers," Israel said. "We could buy one for the back of the truck."

"Well, let's see," Jose said, reviewing the idea. "I catch the fish. You guys buy it in Ensenada. Then you truck it up here to sell. Who knows, maybe the thieves will be buying from us?" Jose offered with a nervous laugh.

"Please do not call them thieves or sharks," Martin replied in defense of his employer. "They are paying the bills, at least for now."

"Why not," Antonio inquired rhetorically. Then, musing with some detachment so as to encourage his friends in a venture he would not pursue because of his newly acquired job as a longshoreman, Antonio said,

"You know I lived near Veracruz on the east coast of Mexico. It is a large and very busy port with some history. It was there that Montezuma's ambassadors first offered gifts of gold to Cortés if he would leave. Cortés kept the gifts and stayed. Later, in the sixteenth century, Manila Galleons filled with silk, spice and ivory from the Orient landed on the Pacific coast. These ships were emptied in Acapulco. The cargo was brought overland to Veracruz on the Atlantic gulf coast. From there, the goods were loaded back on schooners that set sail across the Atlantic for Spain.

"You have a truck and only half as far to go. Why not?" Antonio smiled reassuringly.

Jose, Martin and Israel's imaginations traveled with the mariners from the sea, over the land, and back to the sea. With the Acapulco-Veracruz trade route in mind, Ensenada to San Pedro seemed not only possible but now, so innovatively and intrepidly enticing, it would be cowardice and foolishness not to pursue the plan.

"Your words do carry some weight," Jose quipped, laughing nervously at his big friend.

"Martin, what will you do with all the money we are going to make?" Israel asked.

"I will buy a house. No, two houses; one here and one in Mazatlán. Do you think we might have enough for a sailboat?"

"Why not? But you better start by asking Raul if you can use his truck," Israel advised.

"Can we use the truck?" Martin asked Raul.

"Of course you can use the truck. But for now, it's getting late. Let's see what we think in the morning."

"It is morning," Jose and Laura said at the same time, laughing and giggling nervously together.

The party slowly stood up from the table and stretched as they moved into position to contemplate the completed altar in honor of the dead. Someone had placed Israel's cowboy hat on one of the plastic skulls and had written his name on the jawbone of one of the paper skeletons.

"Who could have done such a thing?" Claudia asked.

"Oh, don't worry. Friends do that: write the names of each other on the skeletons. It is our way of laughing at death," Antonio confessed.

Claudia sighed, overwhelmed by the evening and a little tired, but somehow changed by her cultural immersion. Israel, feeling her empathy, approached, took her hand and looked into her suddenly awakened eyes and said,

"Claudia, I would like to take you to see the musical, *The Man of La Mancha*, based on *Don Quixote*. Or how about joining me for the opera *Don Giovanni*, Mozart's *Don Juan*?"

"I would like that," Claudia said as Israel gallantly kissed her hand to Vanessa's visible disapproval.

Raul thanked all the employees of his restaurant and their guests for coming. Cool air rushed in after each warm hug until everyone had gone home. Locking up, Raul paused by the altar in the still solitude of his restaurant. The marigolds, sweets, candles and skulls on the altar had been joined by pictures of loved ones who had passed on. A black and white photograph of Dolores settled next to a colorful picture of the Sacred Heart of Jesus. Raul knelt in prayer until the sun rose in the East.

Chapter Twelve
A Turtle's Business in Ensenada

A few months later Martin and Israel crossed the international border at Tijuana for the third time in Raul's old blue truck. The rusty bed of the truck, now reinforced and roughly fitted with a refrigeration unit, leaked even when empty. The doors of the truck and the sides of the trailer shone with a flashy new logo: "F3" under a picture of a bluefin tuna and the name *Fresh Fish Fast*.

"If only we had another truck," Martin mused, "we could double our profits."

"That will take a couple of years," Israel responded.

"I know, you told me," Martin said, "but maybe we can think of another way. Now is the time. If only we had another truck."

After another hour's drive, Israel pointed to a sign and said,

"There's the exit for El Sauzal, one kilometer ahead."

Martin turned off Highway One and took the road leading to the port for the commercial fishing fleet.

"It looks like most of the fleet is at sea," Martin observed as the truck weaved its way down to the waterfront. "There would not be so many boats out if the fishing is bad. It must be good."

The truck came to a stop alongside the ships tied to the dock, vessels that vacillated between staying and going with each new swell. Among these, some had their ice-packed holds opened, off-loading their catch.

Martin felt excited at seeing some billed fish and tuna as he stepped out of the truck, jumped from the dock to a tethered ship and climbed up into the pilot house. He radioed the *Saint Augustine* while Israel waited in the truck for a report.

Martin returned ten minutes later and casually sat in the cab next to Israel.

"Well?"

"They're only a quarter full. They won't be back until the morning after tomorrow. What shall we do with the extra day?"

"Let's go to the motel. We'll come back tomorrow," Israel answered, already thinking about what other boats he might approach to make arrangements to augment the yield. The empty blue truck left El Suazal and turned south toward Playa Ensenada on Highway One.

High above Highway One in the colony of *Bellavista*, Eduardo Escobin woke from a siesta. He looked out over the wide sweeping bay of *Todos Santos* through narrow eyes vitiated by sin.

Eduardo Escobin, known as *La Tortuga* for his longevity as a drug kingpin and his slow and calculated movements, resembled a turtle. He always emerged unharmed after a shoot out, like a turtle coming out of its shell after a violent shake up. If any tears appeared on the face of *La Tortuga*, they were a projection from his prey, who often sobbed profusely when brought before him.

La Tortuga lived in a compound so heavily guarded it had to belong to a thief. *La Tortuga* lived with a constant fear of being murdered, a fear felt only by a man who had shed much blood. This fear made him prone to his only emotion, an anger that erupted in fits. *La Tortuga*, after having overindulged every human passion, both according to and contrary to nature, was stimulated by nothing, devoid of all human feelings.

The drug cartel controlled by *La Tortuga* bore his name. The Escobin association oversaw the manufacture of opium, marijuana and methamphetamines in northwestern Mexico and distributed the substances throughout the southwestern United States.

Due to high demand, the cartel's business exceeded all objectives and goals. The only problem, one that Eduardo now thought about as he looked out his window over the Mexican flag and a cruise ship from the United States, was distribution. The cartel had devised a method for moving the drugs over the border without detection but needed a larger fleet of refrigerated trucks.

The leaky blue truck carrying Martin and Israel approached the docked cruise ship and base of the flagpole on its way to the motel in Playa Ensenada. Martin drove as he looked up through the windshield at the gigantic banner.

"They planted the flag there so the cruise ship passengers don't forget what country they're in," Israel joked.

"It's like the flag in Tijuana. It can be seen from miles away, from San Diego," Martin added. "Maybe, so as not to be outdone, someone thought, if we can't build a ship that big, at least we can erect a flag on the same scale, *gigante*! What do the colors and emblem on the flag stand for again?"

"The red symbolizes the blood shed during the battles for independence. The green represents hope and the fertility of the earth. The white did stand for religion until someone changed it to the value of purity."

"What about the eagle?"

"Didn't Vanessa tell you?"

"She might have."

"In the 1300s the Aztecs wandered the lake regions looking for a place to settle. They saw an eagle perched on a cactus devouring a serpent. They saw this as a sign, foretold by an oracle, and made it their capital, today's Mexico City. The Aztecs called themselves *Mexicas*."

"Speaking of places to settle, here is our motel," Martin said as he brought the truck to a stop. The motor started to cool and click as Martin and Israel shut the truck doors. They met the motel receptionist behind a wide, spottily varnished counter covered with paper reservation vouchers and, under glass, faded pictures of game fish hanging from scales. Martin was looking for the key to their usual room in the offset square boxes behind the receptionist when the manager arrived, recognized him, and retrieved the key.

"Will you be staying in room 23?" the manager asked.

"Yes, for two nights this time," Martin replied.

"Have a pleasant stay," the manager said as he handed the key to Martin, who then walked with Israel to the familiar room next to their parked blue truck.

"Maybe we should have asked for a room with an air conditioner," Martin said as placed his duffle bag on the bed next to the bathroom. Israel tossed his cowboy hat on the other bed and opened the window.

"What do you want to do?" Martin asked as he looked at the blank screen of the television.

"It is too hot to stay in here. Let's check out the town," Israel answered, already on his way out the door.

Leaving the motel room, they walked along the city's shoreline avenue toward the cruise-port terminal. As they approached Riviera Avenue, they looked across an inviting garden to an attractive building with a sign in front that read, *Special Exhibit. Free Admission and Wine Tasting Today.*

"It looks like a museum," Martin commented.

"Maybe it is air conditioned," Israel responded. "Let's check it out."

"Why not? Maybe I'll have something to teach Vanessa for a change."

Martin and Israel saw a banner over the entrance that read *Wine and the Gods* and entered the foyer to the museum. Black and white pictures depicting the former exuberance of the building that once was the posh Hotel Playa Riviera hung from the stuccoed brick walls. A discolored poster of the sea erupting from rocks soon occupied Martin's attention as he read aloud:

"The blowhole or *Bufadora*, located beyond *La Banda*, the southernmost point of the *Bay of Todos Santos*, is one of three marine geysers in the world. *La Banda* is to Ensenada what Diamond Head is to Oahu. On the far side of the mountainous point that tapers toward the low estuaries, the blowhole can be imagined as a great blue whale ready to spray from the top of its head."

Israel looked at a vibrant advertisement for a robust wine country to the North of Ensenada with the caption, "Reach beyond the surging waves into the still mountains and try the finest vintages in Mexico."

Leaving the foyer, Martin and Israel walked into a narrow room filled with display cases. The first case contained a copy of a fourth century B.C. image of the Greek god of wine. Dionysus is in ecstasy as he plays the barbiton while two satyrs dance around him. A placard next to the image accredits the god with teaching the Greeks how to cultivate the vine and explains the Dionysian cult as one of ecstasy arrived at through the use of wine and frenzied dancing.

"Are you sure you're not a Greek?" Martin asked with a playful elbow to Israel's side.

"Just call me Zorba," Israel said as he walked on to the next display case that featured a sepia-toned picture of the foundation stones of an old California Mission and an accompanying history telling about how the first vines on the peninsula arrived through the San Ignacio Mission in 1703, planted by the Jesuit priest, Father Juan Ugarte.

Martin, only glancing at the next few displays, leapt in front of Israel and up a short flight of stairs to an upper room and stopped in front of a reproduction of *The Last Supper* by Juan Juanes from the Museo del Prado in Madrid. Martin read from the placards next to the painting:

"At the Last Supper the God-man Jesus Christ instituted the Eucharistic sacrifice of his body and blood: a sacrifice of praise and thanksgiving, of reconciliation and expiation. The Savior of the world did this in order to perpetuate what would be the bloody sacrifice of the cross throughout the ages by the unbloody immolation that takes place on the altar.

"Fray Juan Crespi offered the sacrifice of the Mass in Ensenada for the first time in 1769. Father Junipero Serra, the founder of the Alta California missions, concelebrated. A confrere, Father Bernardino Sahagun, recorded the definitive source of information about Mexico before the conquest in *The Universal History of New Spain*. If what he wrote is accurate, one can understand the impetus the missionaries had for evangelizing.

"While Christians believe that Christ, through his eternally open mortal wounds, is reconciling God and humanity, the Aztecs practiced human sacrifice to keep the heavens and the earth from colliding. While atonement for sin is a dynamic element in the Christian sacrifice, yet, within the ambient of one merciful and loving God, the Aztecs sought to appease many gods."

Israel and Martin arrived at the last display of the exhibit together; a copy of an Aztec sculpture called The Calendar Stone, a solar diadem surrounded by fire serpents. At center, they gaped at what looked like the face of an earth monster bordered by claws grasping human hearts.

"The calendar points to a future cataclysm of the sun fallen to the earth," the placard read. "Human sacrifice and blood offerings on the stone kept the apocalypse in abeyance.

"Tens of thousands of people, usually captives of war, were sacrificed each year by the Aztecs and neighboring tribes. The chests of the victims were opened with a sharp obsidian razor. Then the beating heart was torn out of the victim and held up toward the sun, only to be thrown down at the base of an image to which the temple was dedicated."

After reading about The Calendar Stone, Martin patted Israel on the chest and deftly rushed for a pyramid constructed from stacked cases of wine marking the end of the exhibit. Subsequent to tasting a few of the wines from the vintner sponsoring the exhibit, Martin and Israel left the museum.

Eduardo Escobin squinted out of a window in his *Bellavista* compound. A glass of red wine sat upon a coaster representing the Calendar Stone. Cranky after his siesta, *La Tortuga* became more agitated by the words of Carlos, one of his minions. After listening to Carlos, *La Tortuga* slowly opened his mouth and said,

"You have been there for a week and you only have one truck to show for it."

Carlos had spoken to fifteen drivers at El Sauzal, trying to enlist them into a fleet that transported crystal meth to Los Angeles. He offered the truckers fifty times what they could otherwise make on the same route.

"They get suspicious when I offer the money. They ask around. They find out who we are. They ask what they are carrying. I tell them fish, just like you told me to say." Carlos held his fist in the air, "I'd like to take their trucks and hold them hostage and make the delivery myself."

"I don't want hostages. I want partners! Without a California license and with trucks of our own, we would never pass the border," Eduardo concluded. He dismissed Carlos with a nod and told him,

"Keep trying and don't forget to show them the money. Give them half up front and tell them they will be paid the other half at delivery."

Israel and Martin woke up in their motel in Playa Ensenada the next morning around nine. The sun took a long time to surmount the high coastal peaks, leaving the room they shared cool and subdued.

"I'm going for a swim before it gets too windy," Martin said as he rolled out of bed.

"Okay," Israel replied. "I'll take the truck up to El Sauzal and line up more fish."

"Why don't you wait until I get back? We'll have some breakfast and then go up together." Martin trusted his friend but preferred to drive the truck he borrowed from his father-in-law. Israel didn't feel like waiting and wanted to follow his own pace.

"We could do that. But why not meet for lunch at the Mercado Negro and then decide what to buy based on what I find out this morning," Israel retorted. Martin paused for a moment. Then he picked up the keys to the truck from the bedside stand and tossed them to Israel saying,

"Sounds good. Do you think 12:30 would give you enough time?"

"Yes, I'll pick you up at 12:30."

Changing into his bathing suit, Martin put a towel over his shoulder and left the room. Israel finished dressing by shaping his cowboy hat handsomely over his head and left Playa Ensenada in the blue, leaky truck.

Carlos laughed, blew on the gold and gem rings fastened to his fat fingers and said, "Whata' jalopy," when one of his associates pointed out the arrival of a leaky blue truck at El Sauzal. Nonetheless, he watched the driver closely as he spoke to some of the fishermen. Then, when the driver disappeared into one of the ship's pilothouses, Carlos started to oversee the transfer of a few fish from his vessel to boxes on the shore.

The fish handled by Carlos' associates had already been cleaned and iced. But some had more than frozen water set where the fish guts used to be. These fish had been fitted with crystal meth that looked like ice.

Israel climbed into the pilot house to radio Jose aboard the *St. Augustine*. He learned that the *St. Augustine* was due to arrive at El Sauzal around 5:00 a.m. on the morrow with the hold still a quarter full of fish. Israel disembarked and started to walk the waterfront.

"I saw you drive in," Carlos said as he approached, short and stocky as a tank. "I like the logo on your truck. Are you looking to buy? I've got some fish I need to move in the next day or two and a buyer of my own." Reaching into his pocket, Carlos opened his wallet and started fanning large denominations of pesos.

Israel, initially put off by the aggressiveness of the unknown seller, upon seeing the money, held out his hand to introduce himself.

"My name is Israel." Carlos fumbled with the money. Then he shook Israel's hand and stated his name without making eye contact.

"Yes, I may have some room on my truck tomorrow. It's not very big but I think I'll have room."

"Tomorrow would be good," Carlos replied. "I have a buyer that needs his fish fast, and, hey, that's the name of your company isn't it? Fresh, Fish, Fast? Hee – Hee," Carlos chuckled. Taking the money out again, Carlos held up so much that Israel said,

"My truck isn't that big."

"Oh, you don't need much space. It's just a few boxes. I'll give you this much now. At delivery my buyer will give you the same amount."

Israel looked at the money and thought the proposal was starting to smell fishy. For the first time, he noticed how nicely Carlos dressed compared with the fishermen and dock workers. He saw the rough demeanor of Carlos' associates a few paces away that a smile could not hide.

"I won't know until tomorrow," Israel said. "It depends on how much room we have. Let's see what tomorrow brings."

"We'll be here," Carlos said as he waved the fan of cash before Israel with a bit of acrimony and placed the money back in his wallet.

The impression was not lost on Israel. He felt sorry to let the money go and already turned the proposal over in his mind.

"Good bye."

"See you tomorrow," Carlos answered with the conviction of someone who could spot a flash of avarice in the eyes of anyone.

Israel walked away, back toward the truck, straining himself not to look over his shoulder. The tension within him grew as his past and expectations about the future vied for attention in his deliberations. He thought it might be illegal to transport Carlos' cargo, but asked himself if it would be immoral to take it across the border?

Chapter Thirteen
Raising the Stakes

It was nearly one o'clock when Israel arrived back at the motel in Playa Ensenada. The rationalization for his decision had already taken shape and he made up his mind to transport Carlos' cargo. He decided that if it were drugs, the substance was going to reach the United States one way or another, with or without him. He would not ask Martin for permission nor tell him what had happened, nor what was about to take place.

When he entered the motel room, Israel found Martin sitting in front of the television watching a soccer game with some newspapers spread out nearby.

"What did you find out?"

"The *Saint Augustine* is due in tomorrow morning around five."

"How's the catch?"

"They're one quarter full. They hope to see more fish in the Coronados on their way back. How was your swim?"

"Good. Look what I found in the paper," Martin said as he lifted up a corner of the newspaper for Israel to see.

"This truck is for sale. It only has sixty thousand miles. Do you think we would have enough to buy it and a trailer next year?"

Israel took a glance at the classified ad and replied, "In that amount of time and for that much money we could be driving a semi." Israel brushed the paper aside and said,

"Why don't we get some lunch?"

"You have found something we can agree on," Martin responded.

Over lunch at the *Mercado Negro*, Martin and Israel decided to depart for El Sauzal at 4:30 a.m. and try to be on Highway One by 6:30 a.m. Any later and the heat and traffic at the border would imperil the freshness of their cargo given the poor condition of the leaky cooling system. Returning to the motel, Martin and Israel drank a couple of beers and gambled over a game of dominoes before calling it a day.

Shuteye eluded Israel. Martin availed himself of the chance to fall asleep before his friend's snoring started. Having awakened so late in the morning and, moreover, putting so many questions to himself about what might happen at the border tomorrow and how he would react, Israel accepted a night without slumber but tried to rest his weary mind.

Not once did Israel revisit his decision. He had too much mental discipline or, for the moment, too much spiritual rigidity, to do so. He tried to prepare himself for certain eventualities by asking himself questions. What if the cooler breaks down? What if they unload the cargo for inspection? What if I can't find the delivery spot? What will Carlos do if we are late or the fish rots? After running and rerunning so many "what if" scenarios, Israel finally did get a couple hours of sleep before the alarm buzzed.

The leaky blue truck pulled away from the motel in Playa Ensenada and reached El Sauzal at 5:00 a.m.

"Why don't you go find out where the *Saint Augustine* is. I have to see a seller I met yesterday," Israel said as Martin parked the truck near the waterfront.

"Okay," Martin answered as he walked away from the truck toward the pilot house on the same ship Israel had visited the previous day. Israel returned to the vessel where he spoke to Carlos but no one was there. He didn't want to betray his eagerness so he decided to leave and return later.

Israel walked along the waterfront and waited for Martin's descent from the pilot house. Though dawn, the din of heavy machinery carried across the docks. Israel tried to calm himself by watching a few sea gulls fight over a scrap of fish.

Then a sleek sports car turned onto the waterfront drive and parked next to the blue truck. Carlos emerged from the car and scanned the area. Israel waited. When they made eye contact, Israel gave a slight nod that indicated his willingness to transport the shipment.

Carlos and his associates walked to the boat that served as their office and began loading a pallet with fish, some of which were stuffed with crystal meth.

"They're not going to be back until 6:30 at the earliest," Martin said loudly as he stepped out of the pilot house. "Do you think the coolers will do the job if we leave so late in the day?" Martin asked when he reached Israel.

Israel pondered Martin's question for some time. The stakes seemed to be getting higher.

"Maybe we can buy some blocks of ice along the way to help the refrigeration?" Martin proposed. "I don't want to wait. Our buyers need the fish today."

"So you think it's worth the risk?" Israel asked himself as much as his friend.

"We can afford to lose the fish but I don't want to lose any customers," Martin replied.

"We'll lose both if we don't arrive in time," Israel said as he looked at his watch. It was 5:30.

"The ice will help. Did the *Saint Augustine* catch any more fish?"

"No. They're returning a quarter full," Martin replied.

"While you're getting the ice I'll see about lining up more fish. Can you top off the gas?"

"Sure," Martin agreed. "I'll be back soon," he said as he jogged off to the truck. Once the truck drove away, Israel ran his fingers pensively along the rim of his hat and sauntered over to Carlos.

"So you've made some room for us in that truck of yours?" Carlos asked.

"Yes. We have the room." Israel wanted to ask so many questions. Instead, he waited for Carlos to tell him what he needed to know.

"Where is your friend off to in the truck?"

"He's going for gas."

"You know, your truck seems to leak a little," Carlos observed.

"A little," Israel replied.

"I don't care what time you leave. Our fish will be fine as long as it crosses the border cold. We freeze it anyway. But if you don't keep it frozen, you'll have some problems at the border."

"What kind of problems?" Israel asked.

Carlos returned the inquiry with a glare of hostility. Then composing himself said,

"Let's just say that if the dogs at the border should smell our fish, and they will only smell it if it thaws, we will all suffer for it ..., but especially you. *Comprende*? Don't worry," Carlos said as he gave Israel a pat on the back.

"Where would you like your stuff dropped?" Israel asked as he squirmed under Carlos' touch.

"A few miles after you cross the border a car will pull up next to you. He'll be looking for you once you're on the 805 freeway. He'll honk first, then roll down his window and ask you if you know me. Just say yes and follow him. You'll be going to Long Beach."

The time was 6:30 a.m. when the *St. Augustine* finally rounded the breakwater and arrived at her berth. Martin returned with the truck and sat in the cab with the motor running as Carlos' associates loaded the few wax boxes into the front of the trailer. Israel stacked the frozen blocks of ice around the cargo and pulled the door down.

"Drive on over to the *Augustine*. I'll meet you there," Israel said to Martin. As the truck pulled away, Carlos opened his wallet and filled Israel's outstretched hand with the cold cash.

"There's half now. You'll get the rest on delivery. Don't get lost," Carlos said as he patted Israel on the shoulder again.

"I won't" Israel mumbled, his quick mind already doing the math like an employee earning double time. Israel adjusted the rim of his hat and smiled remorsefully as he walked over to the *St. Augustine*.

Jose's belt buckle flashed in the rising sun as he waved to Israel from the stern of the *St. Augustine*. Israel, on seeing his friend, laughed as he quickened his step. Martin stood by the opened truck. The crew of the *St. Augustine* filled wax boxes with crushed ice and fresh fish.

When Israel arrived at the *St. Augustine*, Jose reached over the rails to embrace his friend. A gold crucifix in a silver anchor swung back and forth from Jose's neck in front of Israel's eyes.

"When did you get that?" Israel asked as he backed away.

Jose stopped his nervous laughter and looked humbly at his friend as he spoke with reverence, his hand cradling the crucifix,

"Jesus protects me."

"Say a prayer for me," Israel requested. "I know it is dangerous on the high seas but you haven't driven on the rough roads for awhile."

Jose felt as eager to catch up with his friends and learn of their business exploits as Martin and Israel were to hear of Jose's ocean adventures. But the temperature was escalating and the ice receded like an Alaskan glacier during a period of global warming with each drop from the blue truck onto the pavement.

"Time to go," Israel firmly informed his friends. It was already 7:30 and 75 degrees when Martin, sitting in the driver's seat, pulled out of El Sauzal onto Baja California Highway One heading north. The "F3" logo on the side of the truck flashed in the sun as swaying heat waves over the asphalt formed a mirage.

Chapter Fourteen
Border Crossing

Martin gripped the steering wheel and floored the leaky blue truck. Meanwhile, Israel shaped and reshaped the brim of his hat. The cab heated as the engine coughed up the hills above *Playas de Tijuana*.

The view offered Martin a momentary reprieve from his anxiety. The green, pink and orange houses piled on each other near the ocean sent a wave of Mazatlán reminiscence through his mind. He could almost hear the snorting suspense in his hometown's dusty arena as he surveyed the bullring on the border's edge.

Israel spied Point Loma on the United States' side of the border. The brown, empty swath of land between him and San Diego seemed to stretch farther apart with every passing second. Israel turned from the distant glimmering glass that soared skyward to the deteriorating cardboard stooped in warren mounds on Mexico's side of the border.

The busy road ran parallel to a sheet metal fence with faded graffiti. The serrated top rose and fell with the undulating topography but always remained the same insurmountable height above ground. The cars and trucks traveled as far North as Highway One could take them. Now, as though caught in a maze, the autos tried to outflank the wall on the eastern front.

Scanning the jagged border through his unrolled window, Israel searched for an opening out of his worry. He remembered the barbed wire that hindered movement across the open range of *Los Altos de Jalisco* during his boyhood. Once he had disregarded its sharp fangs as he tried to pass through its open mouth. He glanced at the biting scars of that entanglement and began tracing the raised mark on his right hand as he wondered if he would make it through the border unscathed.

Israel continued to cycle through mental escapes and topics of conversation. He stopped with the tenacious exploits of the conquistador of Mexico, Hernan Cortés, and smiled at his friend.

"Martin,"

"Yeah?"

"We are like Cortés, running our business the way he conducted his expedition."

"Yeah?"

"He risked it all. When he was in Cuba he mortgaged his estates and exhausted his credit to purchase the ships, weapons and provisions he needed. Would you do that?"

"I'd have to run it by Vanessa," Martin chuckled.

"With just one expedition," Israel said excitingly, "he made a fortune."

"Yah, one trip that took years and cost many lives," Martin added.

"He was no coward. He was on the front line of every battle," Israel said with a slap of his fist on the cracked dashboard of the truck.

"I hope it doesn't take us as long to cross the border as it took Cortés to reach Montezuma," Martin replied.

The leaky blue truck crept along *Avenida Internacional*, still a mile from the Mexican inspection facility. The cab stunk from the perspiration seeping through the porous pits of tight bodies filled with strained nerves. Israel felt boxed in among the trucks making their way under a sign that indicated the queue for loaded commercial vehicles. Rapid, beeping honks filled the noxious air. Israel watched the helmet of a motorcycle cop trying to ride the faded white lines as it approached in his side view mirror.

"There's no turning back now," Israel mused.

"Yeah," Martin said with his attention on the bumper and blinking tail lights of the truck in front of him.

"Wow", Israel exhaled loudly, pounding on the dashboard again.

"What is it?" Martin asked.

"I was just thinking of Cortés again. He burned his own boats, cutting off his only escape, so he and his men could not turn back.

"Cortés discovered a plot by some of his men to return to Veracruz where the ships were at anchor. From there, they planned on setting sail back to Cuba. Cortés spread a story among his troops that the fleet was not seaworthy. He told them that worms had eaten the timbers. He ordered the boats to be stripped of their sails and iron and then he torched them.

"The soldiers threatened mutiny. Cortés said that anyone who would desert their commander and comrades could go back on the one ship spared from the fire and wait until he returned loaded with Aztec gold. He reminded his troops that he made the greatest sacrifice. The fleet was his property, all that he possessed in the world. There was no turning back! The means of escape removed."

Sweat dripped off Israel's face and landed on the vinyl bucket seat of the cab. Stuck in place, a puddle from the drops of melting ice formed on the pot-holed asphalt road underneath the leaky truck. Martin swayed back and forth in his seat as if to will the line forward.

"If we don't get moving, were going to lose the fish," Martin said.

"It is hot in here, but that extra ice will keep the fish cold," Israel replied.

Israel tried to think cool thoughts. His mind wandered back to Cortés' expedition up the frigid mountain passes to the Valley of Mexico. He pictured himself with the small band of soldiers as they passed between *Popocatepetl*, "the hill that smokes", at nearly 18,000 feet and *Iztaccihuatl*, "the white women", a snow-robed summit.

Israel imagined the Valley of Mexico as it had been - terraced pyramids set among majestic mountains. Hanging gardens swayed above an earthen carpet of wild flowers. Aqueducts and canals delivered pure refreshment from the lakes to a patchwork of irrigated fields and sophisticated cities. The air was alive with the buzz of perfumed blossoms.

The Tijuana River Valley on the other side of the border fence, in contrast, appeared to Israel as a flat, barren wasteland. The only running water was directed through sewage pipes and treatment plants. The fecal odor, mingled with the black exhaust of idling trucks, made Israel feel sick again. He swallowed over his impulse to gag.

Israel's hazel eyes searched the blue sky through brown haze. He felt caged in as he thought of the squawk of bright parrots and the flight of songbirds. He remembered the art of feather work and the intricate weave of the dazzling plumage that adorned the Mesoamerican chiefs.

The leaky blue truck finally rolled into the Federal Export Compound in Mexico. Three booths operated at primary inspection.

"The way today is going, I bet we get through Mexican customs only to be held on the other side for hours," Martin predicted. Israel paused for a moment and said,

"It reminds me of Montezuma. Maybe the chief sought to capitalize on the audacity of Cortés by trapping him. He allows Cortés to enter his city without a battle so he can surround him with a multitude of Aztec warriors and cut off his supplies."

"What about Montezuma thinking Cortés' landing was actually Quetzalcoatl's return?" Martin asked. "Here was a tall man with white skin, long dark hair and a flowing beard, just like the god whose return was awaited. He even sent Cortés the headdress of green quetzal feathers from a statue of the feathered serpent," Martin reasoned.

"I don't know if Montezuma had the piety to placate a false god or the genius to trap a political enemy. But soon after he welcomes Cortés he is taken captive. Then Montezuma has to suffer the death of his vassals for following his commands, and the indignity of chains, a prisoner in his own palace, a spectacle to his own subjects."

After almost two hours of waiting, Israel and Martin looped around the secondary inspection facility and rolled to a stop at the Primary Inspection booth.

"Where are you coming from?" the Mexican agent asked.

"El Sauzal," Martin answered. The Mexican agent looked at the "F3" logo with the fish print and asked,

"What are you carrying?"

"Fish," Martin answered. The agent dismissed them with a wave of the hand. The leaky blue truck with its thawing cargo passed the border and entered the United States.

"It all comes down to this. If we get through it will take us twenty minutes. The fish will be fine. If we're stopped and have to go to secondary, it will take more than two hours and we lose the fish," Martin surmised.

"Why not steer for the middle lane," Israel suggested.

Martin and Israel could see the metal overhang that marked Primary Inspection at Otay Mesa. All freight stopped next to the shaded booths that sheltered the custom agents. Without exception, the agents wore mirrored sunglasses.

Joe, the United States agent working the middle open lane, had salt and pepper hair. He considered himself more of a seasoned diplomat than a petty officer. Hour after hour, year after year, he had been shuffled among different booths at disparate borders. Joe had served under dissimilar bosses who were critical of his easy-going attitude. Eventually, the smart supervisors turned to him for advice.

Confronted with daily tip-offs about drug smuggling and human trafficking, Joe still cultivated an open, even welcoming disposition to those who passed by his booth. Fundamentally, he considered the stranger a friend, not a foe. He believed the immigrant to be a contributor, not a taker.

When the leaky blue truck arrived at Joe's booth, he noticed the pale complexion of the two dehydrated passengers. The flashy logo on the trailer didn't fit with the faded condition of the dilapidated vehicle. The seasoned customs agent had already decided to tag the truck for inspection and direct it to secondary. Joe just needed to confirm his judgment with a few questions designed not so much to obtain facts but to detect a person's disposition.

Israel saw the U.S. customs agent smiling and waving to the drivers in the truck ahead. Initially, the behavior confused him.

"He must know them," Martin said.

Israel continued to focus his attention on the gestures of his current adversary, the customs agent. Israel based his strategy on that of Cortés. He thought he could turn an enemy into an ally. Israel recalled Navarez, the Spaniard who came to Veracruz with a superior force to destroy his countryman, Cortés. By surprise, and using the weather to his advantage, Cortés prevailed and augmented his cavalry.

102

Israel realized Cortés never would have conquered Mexico without an alliance with the indigenous people he had vanquished. The courageous warriors of the Tlascalans nearly defeated Cortés before joining forces with him against the Aztecs.

The diplomatic skills of Cortés averted many bloody battles. But the shadow of fear cast by the Aztecs was hard to overcome. Montezuma's enemies were sacrificed or enslaved. Montezuma's vassals, when faced with such threats, tolerated the enlistment of their young men into his army, their maidens into his harem.

The leaky blue truck rolled to a stop in front of the customs booth.

"IDs please," Joe politely commanded. Israel and Martin handed the customs agent their identification. Joe looked from the pictures to the people and asked,

"What's wrong? You look pale."

"I'm worried about our fish. If it doesn't stay cold we'll lose it," Martin responded.

"I guess we are a little thirsty ourselves," Israel joked, trying to copy Joe's magnanimous gestures. The smile left the custom agent's face as he looked at Israel's identification.

"The man in this picture is too handsome. Are you sure it's you?" Joe asked, as he looked through his one-way reflective mirror sunglasses. Israel, too proud of his own good looks, flinched.

"Pull into that line for secondary inspection," Joe said as he pointed his fingers in an arrow. "Just stay in that line. When you get to an open bay, you will need to back the truck in. You can keep the engine and refrigeration running until the inspection begins."

Martin nodded meekly and Israel looked away after the agent handed them back their identification. Martin turned the wheel slightly as the leaky blue truck reemerged into the blaring yellow sun.

"We've lost it!" Martin exclaimed.

Israel felt sick as he looked out his window. A Belgian shepherd dragged its drug enforcement agent toward him. Israel unconsciously held his breath. The moist nose of the dog moved along the underside of the truck and jumped intermittently, like a poodle sniffing the crotch of an unfamiliar visitor. After a minute of watching the canine in the side view mirror, Israel inhaled.

Weakened by the rush of adrenaline, both fight and flight impossible, Israel settled back into the bucket seat, exhausted.

The fanged and barking Belgian Shepherd summoned flashing images of a battle fought by Cortés on the brink of a pyramid dedicated to *Huitzilopotchli*, the Aztec war god.

Israel imagined the life and death struggle that took place on the high slippery stones of the pyramid summit. Many men, locked in mortal combat, rolled off the sides and plunged to their death. At one point, two Aztecs dragged Cortés to the side. Through agility and strength, Cortés freed himself and hurled one of his adversaries over the edge.

The sword of the Spanish cavaliers prevailed after three hours. Rushing the sanctuary of *Huitzilopotchli*, Cortés found its recesses dripping with human blood, Spaniards dismembered and splashed on the walls. They set the shrine on fire, dousing the hellish aura of the Aztec's patron god.

Israel and Martin had been sitting on the edge of the border in the leaky blue truck for two hours when they backed into the United States Secondary Commercial Inspection Facility. Their legs stretched sorely as they stepped out of the cab to open the cargo door. They loitered at the back of the truck talking about their misfortune.

"Today is our *dia de tristeza*," Israel said, referring to the setback Cortés suffered during his retreat from the Aztec city June 30, 1520.

"Just think of what Cortés endured. He led his army, prisoners, and looted treasure over a narrow causeway out of the island city of Mexico. The long caravan started to cross the one and only bridge constructed for passage over three canals. By the time the retreating army was halfway across the first breach, a swarm of canoes surrounded the causeway and a hail of arrows fell upon them. The portable bridge, wedged between the sides of the first opening, could not be moved for transport to the next.

"Those on the brink of the second canal in the causeway plunged into the water to avoid capture. As the carnage continued, the second opening filled with heavy guns, baggage and the dead bodies of the fallen. Those who didn't swim the breach walked over the lifeless debris to the other side. The third gulf stretched the widest. The only way across was to swim.

"Some of the escaping troops sank under the weight of their own greed. Cortés, who a little more than a year before had told Montezuma that the Spaniards had a sickness that only gold could cure, warned his men, on that melancholy night, that he who travels lightest travels safest. Most of the treasure was lost in the water of the lake or left behind.

"Like Cortés, we may have lost our cargo but we still have our lives," Israel said to Martin, knowing that he and his friend might still be imprisoned at any time.

"Yeah, to fight another day, right?"

An inspector from The United States Food and Drug Administration approached.

"Open the cargo door all the way and turn off the engine," the tight-laced officer ordered.

"Do you have your papers?"

"Yeah," Martin said, handing the officer the forms a broker had prepared.

"Where are you coming from?"

"El Sauzal," Israel answered as Martin climbed in the cab to turn the motor off.

"What type of fish are you carrying?"

"We have some fresh swordfish and some frozen yellowtail," Israel responded.

"I need a sample of each," the officer said.

Israel and the officer looked into the back of the small trailer. Closest to them was the swordfish, stacked four boxes high. Hidden from view behind, was the frozen yellowtail stacked three boxes high. One of these boxes, on the bottom, contained fish filled with the crystal form of methamphetamine.

"Stack those two high over there," the officer said, pointing to a place on the platform.

When Martin returned from the cab, he and Israel took a handle on each side of a wax box and lifted the cargo out of the truck. With the truck empty, Israel crossed his arms as the fish lay exposed for inspection.

"Please return to your truck," the officer ordered. "It will take us a few minutes to check for mercury in the fish and traces of anything else."

Israel and Martin jumped down from the loading dock and slumped into the bucket seat in the cab of the truck. Israel, heart pounding, thought of his hero again.

"After Cortés retreated from the capital, his escape to Veracruz was blocked by a multitude of warriors carrying spears. He met them at Otumba, tired and hungry with only twenty horses and no guns. He confided in a comrade that he thought it was his last day."

"Yeah. Then what happened?" Martin asked.

"The warriors were led by a feathered chief, easy to spot with his golden banner. In the heat of the battle, the searching eyes of Cortés found their mark. He ordered his men to follow him in support. They desperately fought their way to the opposing commander. Cortés struck him down with his sword and the warriors dispersed."

"I thought you had told me everything about Cortés. How come you only mention this battle now?" Martin asked.

"Because, today may change a few things," Israel replied.

"I know we lost the fish today. That won't end the business, will it?"

"There is something I haven't told you," Israel said, looking at Martin with one eye and at the side view mirror with the other.

"Yeah?"

"Out of the truck. Come over here please," the officer shouted.

"They must be done with the inspection," Israel said.

"What do you need to tell me?" Martin asked.

"It can wait. Let's see if we can leave now," Israel said as he turned away from Martin and slid out of the cab. Martin stayed in his seat. Israel took a deep breath as he walked to the end of the trailer. He climbed onto the inspection dock.

"Where do you plan on going with this?" the officer asked, holding up and shaking two pieces of fish in a clear plastic bag.

"We are going to San Pedro," Israel responded.

"The inspection is over. Load up and head out. We regret the inconvenience," the officer said.

Martin joined Israel on the platform and together they stacked the boxes of fish back in the truck. Israel stretched for the rope to pull down the trailer door. It closed with a rattle and a bang. Israel reached for the latch and noticed that his hands shook. He moved closer and angled himself so that no one could see him fasten the latch. He jumped back down, took a deep breath, and returned to the cab.

"Let's go," Israel said with a smile of relief. Martin took an inquisitive glance at his friend. The leaky blue truck rolled through the Exit booth and headed west on Otay Mesa road for the northbound 805 California Interstate.

Chapter Fifteen
Fate or Providence

"What were you going to tell me?" Martin insisted. Israel tried to placate his friend with a smile saying,

"Don't worry. I'll get to that." Martin shook his head as he looked from Israel back to Otay Mesa road.

Israel, his mind a little clearer after crossing the border, started speaking freely about Cortés' reconquest of Mexico.

"'I have taken the last step,' Cortés said; 'I have brought you to the goal for which you have so long panted. A few days will place you before the gates of Mexico. We now go forward under the smiles of Providence. Does any one doubt it?'"

"Not Cortés again? You've already told me about the reconquest," Martin pleaded. Israel, with more animation, continued with a theatrical sweep of his hand and a slap on the dashboard.

"'We are fighting the battles of the Faith, fighting for our honor, for riches, for revenge. I have brought you face-to-face with your foe. It is for you to do the rest.'"

Following the leaky blue truck at a distance in a sports car, associates of Carlos identified the "F3" logo flashing in the noonday sun as it merged onto Interstate 805.

Israel, after having been conspicuously quiet and glued to his own side view mirror, looked past Martin through the driver's side window.

"Looking for something?" Martin asked.

"The water."

"It will be on my side. We still have miles to travel before we can see the ocean again," Martin replied.

"Miles. How about the miles that Cortés' soldiers carried the boats through the mountains on their backs. It was four days before they arrived at Lake Tezcuco, the Aztec sea," Israel yarned.

"The boats were carried in pieces. The ironwork, anchors, ropes and sails spared from the burning of the fleet became part of the rigging for the new brigantines.

"In the first naval battle, the ship's sails luffed for want of wind. The Aztec canoes approached by the hundreds. Then a breeze filled the eager Spanish sails. The brigantines rammed the canoes to pieces."

Israel clapped his hands with excitement and pounded the dashboard.

"Please don't do that," Martin said with growing impatience. Israel, knowing Martin's sadness about the siege that strangled the once proud Aztec capital, continued.

"Then Cortés coordinated an advance on the city over the causeways from different directions. This time the soldiers were helped by the navy. The warriors had to fall back from their fortifications as the Spanish cannon, musketeers and crossbow-men advanced breach by breach, block by block into the heart of the city.

"The brigantines formed a naval blockade, beginning a three-month siege on the capital. Cortés offered terms for surrender. Guatemozin, the new Aztec monarch and nephew to Montezuma, refused. On August 13, 1521 Cortés made his final assault on the Aztec capital. Finally Guatemozin gave up, pointing to the hilt of Cortés' sheathed sword saying,

'Better dispatch me with this, and rid me of this life at once.'

'Fear not,' Cortés replied. 'You shall be treated with all honor. You have defended your capital like a brave warrior. A Spaniard knows how to respect valor even in an enemy.'"

Israel paused to relish the moment.

The sports car with Carlos' associates approached in the third lane on Martin's side of the leaky blue truck. Then the driver honked his horn and pulled even.

"What do they want?" Martin asked.

"Do you know Carlos?" the passenger yelled between the moving vehicles.

"They asked me if I know Carlos," Martin said to Israel.

"I know Carlos. Say yes," Israel directed.

"Yes," Martin shouted out his window.

"Follow me," Carlos's associate yelled back.

"He wants me to follow them," Martin said.

"Part of what we're carrying belongs to them. You'd better follow them," Israel said. Martin put on his blinker and fell in behind the sports car saying,

"What's this all about?"

"Now I can tell you what you were better off not knowing before," Israel answered.

"I'm listening," Martin replied.

"What would you say if I told you that after this delivery we will have the money for a down payment on two new trucks and you'll be on your way to buying that sailboat you have always wanted?"

"I'm listening," Martin replied with incredulity.

"As far as I know, we are just carrying a few boxes of frozen tuna," Israel continued. "But judging from the amount we are being paid and for whom we are working, I think there is more than tuna in those boxes."

"Who are we working for?" Martin asked.

"After I agreed to take the cargo, I did some checking. These guys are connected with Eduardo Escobin."

"You mean to tell me we just smuggled drugs across the border?"

"We don't *know* that, and I don't think *we want* to know."

"You do know! Why else would they pay so much?" The question floated through the rushing wind in the cab.

"Why didn't you tell me?" Martin asked.

"You were better off not knowing," Israel replied.

"I won't do it. I'm getting off and we're dumping it!"

Israel had never heard Martin speak in such a tone. He felt the respect he commanded evaporate and intuited that their relationship was changed as he said,

"We can't do that. It would be traced back to us."

"Israel, listen to me! It might be traced back to us, but you will take the fall."

"I don't think a judge will buy that, even with my testimony," Israel advised. "We can't cross these guys now. If I don't deliver, they will kill me, maybe both of us."

"I can't believe it. How could you do this?" Martin yelled.

"You said it yourself; we need more trucks."

"Okay, okay! Just let me think!" For twenty minutes the only sound in the cab was the rushing wind and the laboring engine. As the leaky blue truck completed merging onto Interstate 5, Martin commanded unequivocally,

"Just this once. Never again. Do you understand?"

"Yes, just this once, never again," Israel replied. Then, trying to justify himself before his friend, he said,

"You asked me why I did it. I want to make something of this company. You think someone was going to give us a loan? No. And then, just when we need the money, we get an offer like this. And if you're afraid, don't worry. I've dealt with guys like this before. I know how to handle it. It's Providence."

"Providence. You call this God's plan for us? It sounds more like you fell to the devil's temptation," Martin responded.

"Since when did you get religion? You want to talk about the Bible? You want to talk about good and evil? What about that story, ah, the robe of many colors. You remember, in the book of Genesis. There is Joseph, the youngest and favored son. Then, out of jealousy, his brothers almost kill him. Then, after throwing him in a cistern, they decide to sell him into slavery in Egypt. They dip his tunic in goat's blood so his father thinks he has been torn to pieces by a beast. You remember? Would you say what Joseph's brothers did to him was evil?"

"Yeah," Martin replied, preferring to keep his eyes on the sports car they followed than to look into the eyes of his raving passenger.

"Joseph brought success to his Egyptian master in whatever he did," Israel persisted. "The Lord's blessing was on the Egyptian's house for Joseph's sake, the Bible says. But the master's wife wanted Joseph to lie with her."

"You couldn't leave that part out could you," Martin said.

"But Joseph refused to have sex with her. She accuses him falsely and Joseph is imprisoned. In jail he meets members of the Pharaoh's household and interprets their dreams. A couple of years later Joseph is summoned by the Pharaoh himself for the same purpose. You remember, the seven fat cows and seven skinny cows, seven full ears of corn and seven shriveled."

"Yes, I remember," Martin interjected. "The dream told of seven years of abundance followed by seven years of famine. The Pharaoh puts Joseph in charge of the land. Joseph reserves food during the good years that he then rations in the lean years. The whole world, including Joseph's brothers, come to Egypt for bread. I know the story."

"It was really for the sake of saving lives," Israel continued, "that God sent Joseph to Egypt. Then Joseph cried over each of his brothers before being reunited with his father. What was his father's name again?"

"Jacob," Martin said with a smile.

"Didn't he go by another name? *Israel*."

"Yes," Martin conceded, a little unsure of the affection he felt after having directed his anger toward the same person just moments before.

"You want to talk about Providence," Israel recommenced, relieved at winning back his friend. "I haven't told you about Jeronimo de Aguilar. He was a priest shipwrecked on the Yucatán peninsula eight years before Cortés arrived. Jeronimo, like Joseph in Egypt, became the trusted overseer of an indigenous chief's household. In obedience to his vows, he refused to take a wife."

"Why haven't you married?" Martin quipped.

"The point is, in these eight years, Aguilar learned the Mayan dialects. Now Cortés had left Cozumel in his fleet, only to return because one of the ships had a leak. Miraculously, Aguilar finds Cortés on his return to Cozumel. If it weren't for that leak and Aguilar's shipwreck, Cortés never could have utilized Jeronimo's knowledge of the language in his negotiations with the natives."

"You said Doña Marina was Cortés' translator," Martin objected.

"Yes, both were indispensable to Cortés' success. Marina knew the languages of the Aztecs and the Maya. Aguilar knew Mayan and Spanish. This made it possible for Cortés to communicate with the Aztecs. But she was more than a translator."

"Yes, I know, she was also his mistress," Martin said.

"Yes, but she was also at his side during every meeting with the Indian leaders."

"Vanessa mentioned a quote by Octavio Paz about Doña Marina," Martin struggled to recall. "'That she was a figure representing the Indian's fascination, violation, and seduction by the Spaniards.' Come to think of it, she told me about it while she was talking about you."

"The chiefs gave their daughters to Cortés in marriage. Later, when he became the Captain General of New Spain, he assumed the trappings of power and privilege. He was just doing his part after the ravages of war and disease, and so am I!"

Martin looked at Israel, shook his head, and turned away. Then he started to hear some of Vanessa's warnings about Israel play through his mind. With a straight face he looked back and forth between Israel and the sports car he followed and said firmly,

"Now let me remind you of some of the things you used to tell me about Cortés, about his attraction to Mexico and its people. You used to talk most about Cortés fighting under the banner of the cross."

"Enough," Israel said as he put his head down.

"What about the regulations he made for his army before the conquest," Martin pressed. "'Every soldier is to regard conversion of the peoples as, as, as the ....'"

"'As the prime object of the expedition,'" Israel resumed, "'without which the war would be manifestly unjust, and every acquisition made by it, a robbery.'"

"You told me Cortés was animated by his faith and evangelization was his goal," Martin said. Israel thought for a moment and asked,

"Do you think, sometimes, God might use our baser drives, our desire for money, sex, and power, to motivate us to accomplish his grand designs?"

Both men pondered the question as the ocean appeared on one side of the freeway and the coastal plain on the other. The leaky blue truck passed through Camp Pendleton Marine Force Base. Tanks and helicopters maneuvered in the distance. A small white chapel with a crossed steeple sat motionless.

"I don't know," Martin replied. "What I do know is that Cortés always *informed, consulted and asked* his men before making a move," Martin said with emphasis. Israel took the correction and said,

"I always come back to Cotes' treatment of the people who inhabited Mexico when he arrived. He was cruel in war and generous in peace. He did enslave those who resisted him. But after the conquest he was the advocate and protector of the Indians before the colonists. As governor he would not allow women and children to work; he prohibited the Indians from being used in the mines; he limited a day's labor from sunrise to sunset and he called for Sunday rest.

"I just want to succeed and then I can give something back," Israel said firmly.

"Did you ever think about the people's lives who will be damaged by the drugs we are carrying, all for *our success*?" Martin asked. "What they might have been?"

Israel responded with a blank stare. Martin, feeling again his righteous anger, said,

"No. If you believe in Providence, you are obliged to place your life in God's hands. You took things into your own hands, without regard for God, for me, or the people who are going to be messed up by that poison."

Israel listened to the rebuke but had no rebuttal in the forum of friendship.

"Can we try to make the best of it?" Israel asked after a long pause.

"Yes, but don't fool yourself. You are no Cortés," Martin said. Israel, momentarily hurt by the comment, replied,

"I am not." After a pause Israel continued, "You have to admit, only Providence could have carried Cortés and his five hundred troops to victory over the twenty million people of central Mexico."

"I prefer to think of it as a victory for everyone. I am a *mestizo*, the fruit of the union between the Spaniard and Mesoamerican," Martin replied.

Chapter Sixteen
A Tortuous Partnership

The *St. Augustine* heaved and rolled in the outer waters off Ensenada. Jose's anchor crucifix swung above him as he laid in his musty bunk onboard the ship. Each time his eyes closed, a falling can or a creaking board startled him. He urged the laboring motor to the top of each crest, held his breath when the rumble turned to a purr, and braced himself as the ship raced silently down to the trough.

The same waves that tossed the *St. Augustine* crashed furiously against the breakwater at El Sauzal. The seething sea sucked and spit through the openings in the boulders at the mouth of the harbor. Israel, grinding his teeth and clinching his jaw, sat in the high cab of a new, large white truck parked at the water front. His red eyes darted from road to warehouse and back, watching for Carlos.

Carlos and his associates had been lounging at a cantina on the edge of Highway One when the "F3" logo flashed by like a scintillating decal ironed onto a new white t-shirt.

Martin, having ascended the pilot house of one of the boats at El Sauzal, radioed Jose, who had been nudged out of his bunk and now held the staticky radio.

"Where are you?"

Jose looked at the rocking captain, Lugi, who held the wheel in one hand and reached out with a swaying hand for the radio. With his finger pressing the toggle he said,

"We're full and riding a storm home. At this rate we might be back in around four or five in the morning," the captain guessed, handing the radio back to Jose and putting both hands on the wheel.

Meanwhile, a cloud of dust followed Carlos along the last curve of the narrow road into the port of El Sauzal. Carlos emerged from his car and approached the new white truck as his associates moved toward their floating office.

Israel took a clipboard off the dash next to his cowboy hat and pretended to study it. Carlos reached the truck and rapped his fat, ringed fingers on the cab's door. Israel feigned surprise and slowly rolled down the widow.

"Nice truck," Carlos said in a tone that implied it might just as well be his. "You have some room for my fish?" Carlos asked. Looking down on Carlos from the cab helped Martin respond assertively,

"No. We are full."

"All that room and you cannot find space for me?" Carlos said, pointing at his heart with a voice of nostalgic sarcasm. Then Carlos stepped up on the truck's runner holding the handle and looked eye to eye at Israel saying, "How about you make room."

"I'm sure there are many trucks who would like to make room for you, but I can't," Israel replied, staring back.

"You can't or you won't?" Carlos asked, stepping back down to the ground.

"I can't," Israel responded.

"Maybe we'll have to help you then," Carlos said with a curled lip. Then, glancing involuntary up, Carlos walked away quickly. Israel rolled back up the window and threw the clipboard on the dash.

The door to the pilot house shut loudly behind Martin. Carlos looked up at him before turning away. Walking down the steps, Martin leapt from the boat to the dock and climbed into the cab.

"What happened? What did he say?" Martin asked.

"I suggested he find someone else to move his fish. Then he left. How is the catch?"

"Full, but they won't be here until four or five tomorrow morning. The outer waters are rough," Martin replied as he turned the new white truck south toward Playa Ensenada.

The next morning Martin and Israel returned to El Sauzal to greet the *St. Augustine*. Carlos' car was also there. As the fish from the *St. Augustine* was loaded onto the new, white truck, Carlos and his associates approached Israel.

"Nice truck," Carlos said to those gathered. Then, taking Israel aside, he said, "Eduardo asked me to invite you to his home. It's just a short distance away. Why don't you come with us?"

"I have some fish to deliver. Please thank him but I can't make it today," Israel responded and tried to turn away. Carlos grabbed Israel's forearm and opened his own jacket to show a shoulder-holstered 357 magnum revolver.

"Eduardo does not take no for an answer," Carlos replied. "Don't worry. If all goes well we'll have you back before noon."

Israel followed Carlos to his car and informed Martin where he was being taken and when he hoped to return. Then the sports car left El Sauzal, sped south down highway One and dashed up the coastal mountains to *La Tortuga's* compound in *Bellavista*. A gate barring entrance to the driveway opened automatically. Israel saw two men with AK-47 assault rifles.

"Don't worry. Eduardo treats his partners well," Carlos said as the car wove along a hedged road to the main house. When Israel got out of the car, Carlos told him,

"Lean up against the car. I have to frisk you." Carlos jabbed Israel in the kidneys. Israel's knees buckled under the blow. Then Israel was led down a set of stairs. He looked at the ocean longingly, as if it might be the last time. Then, taken to the bottom floor, he was pushed through a door into a small dark room.

Carlos flipped a switch and an artificial light droned in the windowless room. Israel saw two metal chairs separated by a desk. Stainless steel cabinets lined one wall. Another, shorter side of the room, had a shower head and a nozzle. The other walls, devoid of any pictures or decorations, gave prominence to the electricity outlets. Forced into a cold seat, Israel looked down at a large drain in the middle of the polished cement floor.

"Take off your boots," Carlos demanded. Israel pried off his boots and looked up, wondering what he would be asked to do next.

"I'll be back," Carlos said as he shut and locked the door from the other side.

Israel stood up and circled the desk, tried to open the cabinets, and checked the ceiling for cameras. Instead, he saw a steel track with hooks. After walking around the room again, in the opposite direction, he sat back down, as if to wait for a medical examination from a mad doctor or periodontal procedure from an incompetent dentist. He rubbed his sweaty palms on his pant legs and took a shallow breath through a constricted wind pipe. Israel looked up at the steel hook in the track on the ceiling again and started to shiver uncontrollably. He recalled the torture of Anacleto Gonzalez Flores.

Anacleto, a married man who taught history and literature in Guadalajara during the 1920s, inspired the Cristeros. He advocated a peaceful resistance to the government's persecution of the Church.

Cupping his hands, Israel recalled Anacleto, the writer, hanging from the ceiling by his dislocated thumbs. Israel pushed his lips together as he thought of the orator's smashed mouth and teeth. Israel curled his toes as he imagined the pain of a knife slashing into the tender arches on the bottom of his bare feet.

Anacleto would not divulge the whereabouts of a bishop who went into hiding. He sought to defend his student companions by exclaiming,

"If you want blood, you can have mine!" Soon he was made to bleed not only from cuts on his feet and palms but also from slashes all over his body. Then he was let down. His shoulder was struck with a shattering blow. Anacleto watched as his companions were executed by a firing squad. Anacleto forgave his persecutors and promised to pray for them before being fatally stabbed with a bayonet.

Standing up, Israel took a deep breath, closed his eyes and ran his fingers from his forehead to the nape of his neck, where he rubbed the distended tendons. He did this over and over, as if to try to stimulate thought and relax himself. He stood over the drain and considered relieving himself when the door opened behind him.

"Put on your boots," Carlos ordered. "Eduardo wants to meet you upstairs."

Israel was marched back up the outside staircase to a side door of the compound where another man armed with an AK-47 met him. The guard spoke through an intercom and then the door was opened from the inside. Israel was led into a large room with leather couches, ornate chairs and a coffee table and shown to his seat. He looked through a large window at the giant flag of Mexico and a cruise ship as Carlos stood behind him.

"It's a commanding view, isn't it?" Eduardo, *La Tortuga*, said slowly. Carlos slapped Israel's shoulder, motioning for him to stand up. Eduardo entered the room and shook Israel's hand.

"Carlos, bring us some tomato juice and vodka," Eduardo said. Israel winced.

"Would you prefer soda or orange juice?" Eduardo asked.

"Thank you, soda would be fine," Israel responded. Eduardo walked closer to the window and pointed south.

"Have you heard of LNG?" Eduardo asked.

"No," Israel responded.

"Liquefied natural gas – in a decade or so tankers will be carrying liquefied gas from Russia and Indonesia to a terminal here in Baja. They cool it so that it shrinks, making it easier to ship on the tankers. Once here, the LNG will be converted back into natural gas and pumped through a pipeline to California, Arizona, Nevada, Oregon and Washington. Think of it, the market for energy. The United States' demand for fuel will be supplied from countries across the Pacific. A global network to move a commodity people want and are willing to pay for."

Carlos re-entered the room and presented a tray with soda, juice, ice and vodka and mixed two drinks.

"Have a seat," Eduardo said. Israel sank into a leather sofa and struggled to sit straight. He looked up at Eduardo, who sat in a chair, resting his elbows on its arms. Drink in hand, Eduardo continued,

"Of course, California has nuclear capabilities, a power that can light cities or destroy them, depending on how it is used. But after Chernobyl, no one is going to build more reactors."

Israel, hunched forward, nodded and sipped his soda from a glass he held with two hands.

"Consider the drug market. A few hundred years ago a couple boatloads of Chinese were denied entry into California. So what do they do? They land in Mazatlán and work their way north. But as they go, they sow the poppy seeds they brought with them. Then comes World War II and the Axis powers take over the opium fields in Turkey leaving U.S. soldiers to writhe in pain on the battlefield without morphine. Of course, you know morphine is made from poppies?"

Israel shook his head and reached for the glass coffee table on which to set his drink. He settled back into the couch for a few seconds before leaning forward again, his stomach muscles feeling the strain, so as to listen carefully.

"So the U.S. needs morphine and knows poppies thrive in Mexico. Before long, the two neighbors form an alliance and finance the production of opium. Sinaloa becomes the biggest supplier. But you don't think production would end with the war, do you?"

"No," Israel answered.

"Of course not," Eduardo huffed. "Morphine was used to help put soldiers out of their misery, just as today some choose to use heroin to put themselves out of their own misery," Eduardo said with a long look at Israel, whose agreement he perceived to be insincere.

"Tell me if this is right. I heard that doctors in Oregon, now these are men trained to know the body and heal it, have turned their craft toward killing. It this true?"

"They call it mercy killing," Israel replied.

"You don't need to go to medical school for *that*," Eduardo said in a way that implicated himself.

"Consider methamphetamines. It's purchased over the counter in diet pills so overeaters won't get so hungry. I heard that now, in the United States, the over-consumers don't even worry about diets anymore. They just have the fat sucked out of them and go on gorging themselves. At least the Romans had the sense to vomit away their excess," Eduardo said with a shrug and smile toward Israel, who tried to replicate the gesture.

"Some say that the Americans are only happy when they are shopping. What do you think?"

"I never had the money to shop so I don't know."

"Anyway, the same ephedra used in methamphetamines, also originally from the Far East, stimulates people to work and play like animals weeks on end until they run themselves into the ground. Who am I to tell them not to work and play now and rest later? Whose problem is it that they'll do anything to get the stuff? What am I going to do about it? What are you going to do about it?"

Eduardo stopped and took a deep breath, looking out over the ocean. Then he pointed his beaked nose back to Israel and asked,

"Didn't we pay you enough?"

Israel reached awkwardly for his glass, took a big drink of soda, and set the glass back down.

"I suppose it depends on what we were carrying," Israel answered. Eduardo laughed out loud and repeated Israel's words.

"Carlos, pour me another drink. Do you want anything?"

"I'd like another soda," Israel replied. Eduardo stood up and Israel struggled out of the sofa and stood in place. Eduardo walked over to Israel.

"Relax, I like you, don't worry," Eduardo said as he motioned for Israel to walk with him. They passed through a sliding glass door and stood out on a large balcony. Eduardo pointed to the cruise ship below.

"The Americans come here often. Now they buy what they want, often on credit. Even the government borrows in order to spend. Even though they pay, they are angry about it. Young Mexicans go north to wait on them, to clean up after them, to build for them, to take care of them, to feed them because they have all grown too old to have children of their own. But it is a free country like ours. They can buy whatever they want and they are free to use it as they want. It's their choice. I just give them what they demand."

Carlos arrived with the drinks.

"Why not have a sip of vodka with that soda and add some ice," Eduardo insisted with a look at Carlos, who was already pouring the drink.

"Thank you."

Eduardo and Israel walked to the edge of the balcony. The terrace was suspended above a deep rocky ravine. Israel looked down the steep, stoned chasm and took one hand off his glass and held onto the wrought iron railing.

"Look into that glass," Eduardo said. "What do you see?"

"Water, vodka and ice," Israel responded.

"No, all you see is water and ice," Eduardo corrected. "You know there is vodka but you cannot detect it. When you crossed the border with my fish, you were carrying ice and fish, as far as the inspection agents were concerned. But there was also some meth in crystal form. It is undetectable unless it thaws or is taken into customs."

"But they did check a box from your load when we crossed the border," Israel said.

"That doesn't usually happen," Eduardo replied.

"They must have checked the wrong box," Israel said.

"They don't check any more than twenty percent of the cargo crossing the border," Eduardo explained. "With the new truck the shipment will stay cold. You won't look so suspicious and you'll be relaxed. You will have room for more cargo so the chance of detection is reduced and I can pay you more. Did I not pay you enough last time?"

"Yes, you paid me fairly," Israel said as he looked out over the ocean. "I just cannot take the risk again. I'm willing to pay you back, if you can give me some time, but I cannot take the risk again," Israel pleaded with a glance down the ravine.

"Business is all about risk. We would assume the risk together and share the profits. Imagine not just one new truck but a whole fleet of them," Eduardo cajoled.

The two men were quiet as they stood on the terrace. In the corner was a large red clay pot with pomegranates ready to burst. At the base, ants devoured a grasshopper. With each passing second Israel could feel the rapport between Eduardo and him evaporate in the dry, hot air. Eduardo studied Israel intently and said,

"As a partner, I've entrusted you with our methods. How can I know you will not inform others? If you remain my partner," Eduardo said, gripping Israel's forearm, "you will take risks, and make money. If not, you're at risk and for nothing." Eduardo finished his drink in a gulp, took Israel's glass, and said,

"It's getting warm. Let's go inside." Israel followed.

"Mr. Escobar," Israel started.

"No. Call me Eduardo."

"Eduardo, there is much I do not know about business that I will learn in partnership with you. Thank you for your confidence. Before we formally resume our partnership, I need to prevail upon your generosity."

"Please, sit down here," Eduardo said, motioning Israel into an armed chair he pulled up near his own. Sitting down, Israel continued his proposition.

"I have two new trucks thanks to you and my current colleague."

"Oh, yes, Martin is his name."

"Yes. He does not know your, I mean, our methods. He has narrow ideas and limited needs. But I owe him much. With your permission, I'll break off my ties with him and start my own company under a different name. But I wish to allow him to keep one of the trucks and know that you will respect his decision and ensure his safety."

"Fine. We will make sure you have the trucks you need. When do you foresee making the next delivery?"

"Permit me six months. I need to find an American citizen with whom to enter into a contract for civil marriage, form the new company and hire a couple of drivers."

"No church wedding?"

"Only if I decide to love her."

"Fine," Eduardo said. Then he yelled, "Carlos, come here!" Carlos stood at Eduardo's side. "Take my new partner back to El Sauzal."

Israel was led out of the house, escorted through a gauntlet of AK-47s, and stuffed back into the sports car. The gate at *Bellavista* opened and Israel looked up at the ocean with relief. His hazel eyes remained fixed on the blue sea for the remainder of the trip back to El Sauzal.

Martin and Jose, after having loaded the trailer with four pallets of fish, sat in the cab of the new white truck waiting nervously for Israel. They laughed uneasily as Jose described some of the foibles of his shipmates. Most of all, they spoke about fishing. As high noon approached, Martin showed Jose a picture of himself, Vanessa and their two children.

"That is Luke. He is almost two years old now."

"Who's that?" Jose asked.

"Isaac. He's just seven months."

The time was half past noon when Israel was dropped off at the waterfront.

"We began to wonder if you would make it back," Jose said.

"So did I. Let's go while the fish is still fresh. Goodbye, Jose," Israel said as if it was for the last time. Jose uttered a nervous laugh and waved goodbye.

Chapter Seventeen
Another Decade to Catalina

"Dad, it's getting hot. I'm going to change."

"Okay, son." Luke took off his sweater when he heard the captain say,

"Bring up the binoculars."

Luke responded with the eagerness of an eleven-year-old to the command. He reached for the binoculars hanging on a hook above the navigation table. Then he scaled the four weathered wooden steps of the companion way and delivered the binoculars to his dad who sat comfortably at the helm.

Martin was both father and captain to his son while they were aboard his thirty-four foot sailboat, *Precise Intuition*. The name of the vessel had been inspired by the art and science of navigation. Martin wanted to know where he was when at sea, for it had not always been that way.

Twelve years earlier, Martin was a stowaway on a ship that traversed these same Pacific waters along the northwise shipping lane between Santa Catalina Island and the Southern California coast. He had cramped himself in with a cargo of canned shrimp and was carried from Mazatlán, Mexico to the Port of San Pedro. He had known the destination, but after nine days in the hold he was dehydrated, disoriented and driven to despair.

Now Martin, filled with hope, sipped cool water and gazed at Frog Rock through his binoculars. He knew his position exactly. The boat reached on a course of 290 degrees toward Hen Rock along the leeward side of Catalina. Martin eased the jib sheet as rays of sun bounced along the staysail. Luke bounded across the foredeck in shorts and a t-shirt, happy to be close to shore and trying to wake up his two younger brothers still asleep below.

"Luke, hand me the chart."

"It's right next to you, dad."

Martin found the chart and spread it on a teak table that he extended from its folded position near the large wheel and compass. Luke stood on the seat and leaned over his father's shoulder.

"Let's see, three fathoms of depth here, two there," Martin mumbled as Luke reached for the binoculars.

Luke called on his sea legs to match the rhythm of the swells as he steadied himself to spy the island cliffs.

"Watch the boom," his dad warned.

"Don't worry, dad."

Scanning the cliffs again, Luke saw a large bird. He lowered the binoculars and looked. Returning the glasses to his eyes, he yelled,

"A bald eagle! A bald eagle!" as his heart soared with the bird's flight. Martin pushed himself away from the chart and asked,

"Where?"

"See," Luke pointed, "over there," as his finger traced a line in the sky.

"Oh, I see it now," Martin said with awe. He felt a tinge of patriotism, a sentiment quite foreign to him, as he fixed his blue-grey eyes on the large wingspan of the eagle. He could not understand the fanatic nationalism of the Mexicans who cheered for a soccer team nor the Americans who stood so solemnly for the pledge of allegiance to a flag. The thread woven into his make-up did not stitch him to a country but to the land that sustained his family for generations.

Luke's pounding on the deck did not awaken his brothers but it did obtain his mother's attention. Martin's gaze at the soaring white-plumed bird then fell upon his graceful wife, Vanessa. As she approached to kiss him on the forehead, she leaned over. A light breath of air slipped beneath her white cotton dress and lapped the tanned valley between her smooth breasts. Vanessa's big brown eyes met Martin's with familiar yet evocative affection.

"Good morning, hon," she said as she turned with a wave of her long, shiny, black hair. Martin playfully tugged at a handful of dark hair, slowing her turn and drawing her back to him. He placed his arm around her slim waist, resting it on her wide hips, so as to acknowledge the effect her morning greeting had on him. Martin knew this touch might be the last one of the day. He reluctantly let Vanessa go as the little ones emerged from their bunks.

The sun had not arrived at its zenith when *Precise Intuition* sailed by Hen Rock and rounded Long Point. The cliffs above Italian Gardens plunged deeply into the Mayan blue sea as Martin heard a bellowing sound.

"Do you hear that?" he asked Andrew, the youngest of his three sons, who wiggled at his side.

"What?"

"Listen."

Then a sound deeper than a bass bassoon traveled a narrow valley from an inland prairie to their open ears.

"I heard it!" Andrew cried, clutching his dad's legs with both arms asking,

"What is it?"

"A buffalo," Martin answered. "Go get the binoculars and keep a look out." Martin knew Andrew would not see a buffalo two to three miles away but the distraction would allow him to return to his charts.

Immersion in the tasks of navigation helped a man, who had only known work, transition into relaxation.

"What are buffalo doing on an island? Did they swim over?" Luke asked.

"They were brought over years ago for the filming of a movie and never left," Vanessa replied.

"Where's the buffalo?" Andrew started asking over and over again.

"That's the hundredth time you've asked," Isaac, the middle child, said.

"Son, we might not be able to see a buffalo just yet," Martin conceded, regretting the decoy. Andrew accepted the explanation and turned his boundless energy on his brother. He stamped his front leg, hunched over, and, making horns out of his fingers, took repeated charges at Isaac. Then Luke entered the fray and wrestled the buffalo to the deck by the horns. Andrew lay on his side, fingers still on his head, bellowing as best he could, turning from side to side like a bison taking a dust bath.

"No, no," Andrew laughed as his brothers tickled him.

"There's a buffalo on this boat right now!" Martin said loudly. The boys stopped and gathered around their dad.

"It's grilled and ready to be covered with tomatoes and onions on two pieces of bread."

"Now they're not going to eat them," Vanessa said as she landed a firm punch on Martin's shoulder.

"When they get hungry enough, they'll eat'em," retorted Martin.

"Ugh, we're going to eat buffalo burgers?" Isaac winced.

"Why not? It's as tasty and has more vitamins and less fat and cholesterol than beef," Vanessa explained. "Who is going to be the first to try one?"

"I will," Andrew said with a sheepish voice.

"Good. Come help me with lunch."

Luke and Isaac went to assist their mother while Andrew stayed behind to enjoy his father's undivided attention.

Below deck, there was a small table and kitchenette. The cushions around the table were piled with jackets and sweats that the boys had shed during the morning. The dark wood interior of the cabin made the cramped quarters feel a little more luxurious.

Vanessa retrieved sandwiches and green and red grapes from the icebox. Meanwhile, Luke and Isaac fought over who would open a bag of potato chips. Isaac squeezed and the bag opened from the bottom with a pop. Luke thrust his hands under the bag to stop the avalanche of chips until Vanessa found a bowl.

"That's enough. Go take your dad a drink." The boys respectfully complied and then charged up the stairs to the deck, each with a can in hand.

When the last salted chip had been eaten and only a few grapes remained on the vine, the buffalo burgers devoured, and the belching contest ended, the family took a satiated pause. The break from activity was cut short by Isaac and Andrew, who balanced themselves along the life lines and walked to the bow pulpit, ready to preach to the dolphins or whiskered seals if they would listen. Sitting down, they waved their feet just above the reach of the jumping water.

"Take the wheel, Luke," Martin ordered.

"Let me get my hat first," Luke replied, returning to the helm out of breath but with the cap that his dad had given him.

Luke always wore the hat when he steered the boat. The bill of the cap, stiff as a pelican's beak, shaded Luke's eyes and nose. The rest of the hat covered his head softly and fit firmly enough to withstand most winds.

Vanessa and Martin sat across from each other. Vanessa watched Luke and said,

"He looks like you at the helm, the way he studies the water and blinks his eyes." Martin observed the birthmark on the underside of Luke's arm and the matching shape on his own and remembered the same mark on the underside of his dad's arm.

Luke had just enough of his mother's features for Martin to love him dearly and just enough of his own characteristics to help him like himself. Martin wondered if Luke would thank him later for his part in bringing him into humanity.

The ebb and flow of Martin's thoughts, like a current influencing a course, moved his mind to action. He reached beyond himself and caressed his wife's warm shoulder. Bolstered by the stimulus of this touch, he planned an equally grand but more complicated endeavor. The words to rouse his crew and carry the ship from Goat Harbor seaward splashed from his mind.

"Prepare to come about."

"Where are we going?" Luke asked.

"Where are we going?" Martin repeated. "Should we not first ask from whence we have come?" Martin continued with a philosophical smirk. And like Aeneas, of Virgil's ancient *Odyssey*, Martin studied the winds and cupped his ears to catch the movements of the air.

"The seas offshore look promising! Trust the captain and follow orders, mates and madam!"

Laughing, the rest of the family hurried into position.

"Mind your hooves, landlubbers," Martin warned with a look at Luke who was poised near the port side winch. "Do you know why they call it Goat Harbor?"

134

"Because there are goats on the cliffs above," Luke inducted.

"You're right. On occasion, however, one of those sure-footed goats has a misstep and falls from the cliffs above with a fatal splash below. So watch your head and mind your feet so you don't fall overboard."

"Ready about?"

"Ready," replied the crew.

"Helms Alee!" Martin exclaimed as he turned the wheel. Vanessa guided the boom. Luke released the jib sheet on one side and then, crossing to the starboard side, trimmed the jib with coffee grinder turns on the winch handle. *Precise Intuition* completed her turn and pointed toward the open sea.

The tack complete and the sails trimmed nicely, Martin briefed the crew on the float plan.

"We'll make a few tacks as we head offshore and then we'll set the spinnaker and return to Hen Rock, our anchorage for the night." Martin studied the faces of the crew for feedback. Most importantly to him, Vanessa gave her blessing with a hesitant nod.

After *Precise Intuition* zigzagged for the fifth time, Vanessa sighed loudly and wiped her moist brow. Luke sweat from his work in trimming the sails and his arms shook from his cranks on the winch. Deciding to remain on course and grant the crew time to recuperate before setting the spinnaker, Martin simply said,

"Let's build up some boat speed."

Looking over his shoulder, beyond the dingy tied to the stern, Martin traced the course they had sailed, so calm was the water. He also studied the island that now appeared as a silhouette even though the sun was still well above the east summit. A flying fish darted by and an old impulse nearly caused Martin to set a trolling rod for Dorado, or Mahi Mahi as the Hawaiians call it. Instead, Martin put on his glasses, knowing the sun would shortly be in their eyes, and looked up at the masthead fly for a reading on the wind direction.

"Prepare to jibe!"

Vanessa pulled on the main sheet. When the boom reached the middle of the boat, Martin yelled,

"Jibe Ho!" and turned the boat away from the open sea for a down wind jaunt toward the beckoning bays of Catalina.

Butterflies stirred in Luke's stomach. His dad was about to send him to the foredeck to help set the pole. He rehearsed the impending challenge in his mind. Pulses of exhilaration at remembering the sight of the parachute sail flying high overcame the trepidation he felt at the prospect of setting the pole and getting the sail airborne.

"We are going to hoist the spinnaker. Madam, please take the wheel," Martin commanded suppliantly.

"First mate, go forward and I'll hand up the sail." Martin went below, opened the hatch, and pushed the sail through. After returning to deck, Martin and Luke raised the spinnaker pole. Without waiting for further instructions, Luke retrieved and fastened the spinnaker halyard to the head of the sail.

"Okay, Luke, go back and set the aft-guy," Martin tried to say calmly.

"Okay, dad," Luke responded as he scampered across the deck, resembling a large bug with his sunglasses and disproportionately big hands and feet.

"Ready?"

"Yes."

Martin began hoisting the spinnaker halyard hand over hand near the mast.

"Hold'em even, son," Martin directed, referring to the corners of the sails as the head climbed skyward. Then, with building suspense, Isaac and Andrew gasped as the large image of a fish print unwrapped above their cricked necks on the canvas of the sail.

"Let her fly!" Martin exclaimed.

Then the red letter and number "F3" unfolded on the spinnaker below a picture of a blue fish. The sail gently filled and pushed *Precise Intuition* toward Catalina Island.

Chapter Eighteen
A Stranger in Paradise

The scrub-brushed land of Catalina rises from the Pacific sea where the winsome town of Avalon mingles with a crescent shore. The Casino, the icon of the island city, attracts visitors even without the teasing tumble of dotted bones or the clicking spin of striped wheels. The Casino feels as safe to people who have gambled everything and lost, as it feels exciting to those who have never risked a dime.

Having made some bad decisions, Judy was losing at the game of life. She purchased her ticket for the ferry to Catalina Island first, but boarded last. Judy watched as the strangers standing next to her on the *Sea Horse Express* waved to unfamiliar persons lining the dock in San Pedro. Finally, a horn blew and the deck vibrated to the machinations of engine pistons and propeller revolutions.

Reaching into her purse, Judy grabbed a pack of chewing gum and placed a stick of spearmint into her mouth. Then she neatly folded the silver foil and tucked it into the pocket of her shorts. Judy tried to rub the goose bumps off her closely shaved bare legs even as they tanned in the sun.

Soon, the onrushing wind made Judy's eyes water. Splashes cascaded from the bow into a spray that dripped through her outstretched fingers. Still, she remained as transfixed by the water as her greasy, bleached hair stayed unmoved by the wind. Shaking, Judy unzipped her backpack and pulled a pair of sweatpants over her shorts.

Judy's feet cried for rest. She didn't care about the ingrown nail on her big toe any more because she no longer felt it. The arches that supported her through the busy hours of part-time jobs at a diner and two fast food restaurants hurt. Too many restless thoughts and fiery impulses burdened Judy's weary mind, leaving her brain as numb as her feet.

A commotion stirred behind Judy. Uneasily, she looked over her shoulder. A man kept pointing a finger in her direction.

"Why is everyone staring at me?" Judy asked herself.

"They are all smiling. They must not be watching me," Judy concluded. Then she peeked over her other shoulder. Her fears were momentarily left behind and distant hopes fleetingly realized. Catalina materialized from behind a shroud of haze.

The *Sea Horse Express* seemed to approach Avalon more quickly when The Casino came into sight. More of the passengers climbed to the upper deck with such anticipation that they may as well have been spectators chosen to watch the Greco-Roman gods at play. And Aeolus was touching the top of Poseidon's realm with intermittent brushes of white that briefly capped the surface of one blue wave before jumping to the next swell.

Judy tried to avoid contact with the other passengers who brushed up against her even as she searched for something to wrap herself around. Judy fixated on the red tile dome of The Casino rising toward her. She imagined herself on the balcony looking through the narrow gothic windows. Once inside of the grand ballroom, she hummed a waltz. She fancied herself as a girl wearing pink slippers again, gliding over the dizzying parquet dance floor. Then the big band horns sounded in Judy's head to a beat that made her as jittery as a bug.

The revelry stopped with a bump as the cattle boat, a nickname frequently applied to the ferry, reached its stall. Judy, who was as skinny as a rope, felt lassoed by the horde of sweaty obesity that pressed upon her. Rounded up with the rest of the clamoring crowd, Judy funneled through a gate and down a ramp. The stampede jostled toward the bay side restaurants without her.

Judy craved something food couldn't satisfy. She spit out her stale white gum and settled for a fresh green piece. The familiar flavor didn't alleviate Judy's feeling of being a stranger in paradise. The Casino, however, seemed to call her by name. Judy walked with lengthening strides and high swinging arms along Casino Way.

The boats bobbing at their canned births in Avalon Harbor appeared to Judy like so many floating toys next to the sturdy immensity of The Casino. The edifice, though mellowed by the ageless sun, stood with an enduring virulence. Wheezing, Judy reached the shaded side of the landmark and touched the cool stucco. She stroked the art deco accents that emerged on the body of the building and felt a gaiety long forgotten.

Turning back, Judy walked more slowly along Casino Way. She noticed the Catalina tiles depicting the island's history. Beautifully colored people, with the best claim to indigenousness, stood along what they called The Bay of Seven Moons. Other squared images told the story of gold miners, otter trappers and fishermen. There were no painted clay pictures dedicated to the bootleggers and drug smugglers Judy had read about.

Vendors sold candy, cigarettes, and beer along the waterfront. Judy scampered by the stores and cafes even as she heard her stomach growl for the first time in days. The new object of Judy's attention, The Pleasure Peer, held out the possibility of walking on water.

Arriving at the peer, Judy hesitated. After just a few paces along the wooden planks, she stopped to peer over the side.

140

Bright orange Garibaldi, California's state fish, swayed with the current. The sandy bottom below the overgrown goldfish shimmered through the emerald water like the green palm fronds high above.

Resuming her walk down the planks of the pier, Judy passed a scuba diving shop. She paused, spit into a trash can, and took another stick of spearmint gum from its wrapper. She saw a yellow submarine and came to a window where one could purchase a ride on a glass bottom boat to Lover's Cove.

Judy did not want to know what dwelt in the depths. She feared that if she went underneath she might not find the surface again. Her tennis shoes creaked over the wood. She did not want to look between the cracks at the monsters that might be lurking below. She tried to calm herself,

"Easy. What are you so panicky about? It's not even dark yet."

Judy lost herself in the piercing eyes of a pigeon as the island visitors around her bobbed their heads so as not to miss any amusement. The smell of vinegar revived Judy. She sighed and continued her walk down the planks to the green, white-trimmed building that seemed to hold her fate at the end of the pier.

Fish and Chips, a sign read. Judy stepped in some ketchup as she ordered the specialty of the house. She reluctantly took the fresh piece of Wrigley's out of her mouth, retrieved the foiled paper from her pocket, and carefully placed the gum in the wrapper. She nibbled at her breaded fish and salty French fries from a barstool overlooking the bay and The Casino.

The Grand Opening of Avalon's Casino took place in 1929. Big bands performed in the ballroom while silent motion pictures played on the screen in the theater below. The owners did not mind if the patrons stuck chewing gum under the seats. The Casino was built on bubble gum. A year after William Wrigley, Jr. purchased Catalina Island, he bought the Chicago Cubs. The baseball team held Spring Training in Avalon during the roaring twenties, somber thirties and part of the embattled forties.

The din of baseballs hit by lumber bats gave way to strokes of iron and an occasional shout of "Fore." Not far from the old grass diamond field, now a golf course and fire station, Father John walked between a couple of pews in Saint Catherine of Alexandria Church.

Father John's fingers imbedded in a warm, sticky mold as he reached down to put a kneeler back in place. He grimaced and just managed to refrain from cursing Wrigley for ever making gum.

Father John's broad shoulders and thick legs gave him the appearance of a baseball catcher. He preached with the precision of a big league pitcher. Father John possessed a repertoire of skills for helping people solve their personal problems like that of a caddie holding a golf bag filled with an assortment of wedges, drivers and putters.

"Hi, Father," a voice rang out. "What time is Mass tomorrow?" Father John wiped his hands on his pants, stood tall, humbly laughed at himself and turned to greet the visitor. The priest was not offended that the young man who asked the question wore shorts and flip flops that clicked through the church. Father John, accustomed to beach community etiquette, wore sandals himself.

"The first one is at 9:00 o'clock in the morning."

"Thank you," the young man said as he reached to take the priest's outstretched hand. "Father, I was just wondering, are the church and the island named after the same person?"

"Yes. Viscaino arrived here in November of 1603, on or near the memorial of Santa Catalina in the Roman martyrology. The Spaniard named the island in her honor. He must have been inspired by the courage of the fourth century woman."

"What'd she do?" the young visitor asked.

"Legend has it that Saint Catherine of Alexandria denounced Emperor Maxentius, in person, for his persecution. The Emperor put her in jail and then left the city. When he returned, his own wife, the Empress herself, along with hundreds of soldiers, had become Christians! The Emperor had them all put to death. Saint Catherine was beheaded. Saint Catherine..."

"Pray for us," the young visitor responded, framed in the colored light of a stained glass window. "See you tomorrow."

"See you then," Father John confirmed with a smile.

Leaving the church through a side door, Father John entered a courtyard of contemplation. Water trickled from a fountain. Pink bougainvillea climbed over walls that waved with shadows and light from a yellow Hesperia tree. Father John sat down on a bench and stared at the leaves of a fern, the tips browned by the sun. Chimes from a distant hill settled soothingly on the late afternoon air.

Father John, often referred to as the padre, moved indoors. The padre turned on the radio and reclined in a well-worn easy chair. Guitar strums from *Espanola's Danza Triste* by Enrique Granados filled the room with joyful music. After the last note, the voice of a disk jockey introduced the next song.

"Summer, concerto in G Minor Opus Eight Number Two, Presto, composed by Vivaldi and conducted by Toscanini."

The padre, already enthusiastic about an approaching visit with some friends, smiled proudly that Vivaldi was a priest too.

He waved his hands in the air to the music as the rocking recliner squeaked under him. Anticipating the interplay of the notes, the padre continued to pretend he was conducting the classical score from a clear beginning to a unified, climactic end.

Father John reached for the radio dial at the conclusion of the song and searched for a jazz station to prepare for the festival. His friends, the Harmonds, were due to arrive soon. They planned to meet at the rectory of Saint Catherine's and walk to The Casino for the jazz festival together.

The sound of a saxophone indicated that he had found the station. Fr. John tapped his feet to the beat, admiring how the band's percussionists and wind instruments started a repetitive chord only to be joined by a dissonant chord of emerging melodies and parting beats. He considered jazz the quintessential expression of what people called Post-Modernism; without a unifying center, the goal, if one existed, was to live from moment to moment.

The padre turned back to the classical music station and relaxed in the recliner. He savored a glass of cabernet sauvignon as it moistened his palette. He fell asleep thinking, that if he did doze off, it would be the Harmonds' knock on the back door that would wake him.

Judy fed the last of her French fries to the pigeons and took the foil off her moist wad of chewed gum. Then she stepped off her barstool and strolled back down the pier. When she arrived at the place where the wooden planks met the sandy beach, she untied her tennis shoes and pulled off her socks. She walked over a few beach towels and ducked under a pair of colorful umbrellas. Judy smelled coconut butter mixed with diesel fuel near the water's edge. She heard the shrill cries of swimmers and the boom of cannonballs interspersed with the buzz of amphibious inflatables used by private boat owners to infiltrate the city of Avalon.

Little waves slapped at Judy's ankles as she walked along the beach. Eventually, she found a spot to claim for herself. She sat down, using the trunk of a palm tree for a backrest. She dug her heels into the sand as if grinding roots in a pestle. Judy looked at The Casino; with so many beach toys and sand castles dotting the shore, it appeared to her like a giant top or a tower of Camelot.

Glancing from The Casino and scanning the harbor, Judy noticed the flippant names painted on the stern of moored yachts: *KarmaKazi*, *ReelTime*, *PipeDream*. The masts of the sailboats moved from side to side like a metronome that carried a lullaby that rocked Judy slowly to sleep. While Judy slumbered, beach towels rolled and dresses fell over bikinis. Chairs folded as umbrellas closed for the day.

Judy awoke from her nap to the subdued rays of a setting sun that futilely tried to warm the cooling sand. The crowd had retreated from the beach as dusk hovered over the sea. She could feel the fear rising with the moon and her heart sinking with the tide.

Judy heard laughter from the bayside bars behind her. Moaning, Judy picked herself up and turned to see people huddled together over pitchers of beer, each drowning his own sorrow in a mug of ale. Judy wondered how it would feel to jump from the steep cliffs into the salty sea.

Stuffing her socks into her backpack, Judy slowly put on her tennis shoes. She walked toward the lighted street and crescent promenade. She wanted to run but could only walk lethargically. The anonymous crowd drew Judy into its midst and carried her down Catalina Avenue. She walked straight ahead as couples gradually peeled off toward their hotel rooms. The few people who remained around Judy began disappearing behind the doors of their own homes. Erie hues cast by television screens flickered through shuttered windows.

The grade of the empty street steepened. To her left, Judy saw the open lobby of a quaint inn. The receptionist smiled over the hotel register. When Judy approached, the receptionist's smile turned to a frown.

"I'm sorry, no vacancy; we're full."

"Is there a church nearby?" Judy asked.

"Yes," the receptionist answered and escorted Judy outside saying, "Go straight and make a left on Beacon Street."

Judy followed the directions and studied the street signs. She arrived at Beacon Street and a tinge of hope emerged as she stood on the corner. She remembered that in the past, on desperate nights like this, she found a familial welcome at a house of prayer that provided assistance to her like a safe harbor sheltering boats from a storm.

Judy peered down the street but could not see a church. Nonetheless, she still continued to go forward, trusting that the words spoken to her were true. A few paces later she saw a bell tower shining beyond a sign that read *Saint Catherine of Alexandria Church*. The inviting sound of a fountain drew Judy into a courtyard toward the rectory. Looking between the branches of a hibiscus, she could see the water faucet for a kitchen sink and a few abalone shells filled with soap on the window sill. Judy saw a door and feebly pounded her palms against it. She knocked again and the hollow quiet that echoed back made her feel empty. Panic started to fill the void when Judy saw a sign that read,

"Please kindly use the front door."

Father John heard the faint knock on the back door. He arose from his recliner to greet his friends. When the brass hinges swung open, a person was turning away. Father John, surprised to see the solitary figure and not the expected couple, asked awkwardly,

"Oh, do you have an emergency?" He was ready to ask the person with her back to him to call for an appointment on Monday. The face that turned on Father John looked like the subject of Edvard Munch's *The Scream*. Large white eyes in jaundiced skin stood out against the dark blue sky beyond.

"I don't know," Judy answered, on the verge of tears, when she detected the hurried speech of the priest. She looked down as she stood on the door step.

Shaken by the appearance of the woman, Father John surrendered his own plans for the evening and asked,

"What is your name?"

"Judy."

"Please wait for a moment by the fountain and I'll be right back."

The padre scribbled a note, "Go on ahead without me. I'll meet you at The Casino later." He tacked the note onto the back door of the rectory for the Harmonds. Then he returned to Judy at the fountain and saw a star twinkling over her shoulder and said a little prayer wishing for patience.

"Follow me." Together they walked to the front door of the rectory where the priest kept a simple office.

"Please take a seat." Judy slumped into a chair. The priest sat down at the round table across from Judy and introduced himself.

"Let us pray," the priest suggested with open hands and a heart that already burned with empathy. Judy glanced up briefly and turned her little hands up too.

"Heavenly Father, send the light of your wisdom and Spirit of consolation into our troubled minds and broken hearts. Grant Judy healing and peace. We ask this through Christ, our Lord. Amen."

An open silence filled with possibilities ensued. Usually those sitting at the other side of the table started to talk so fast and so long that the doctor of souls could listen for signs that allowed him to assess surface problems and underlying issues. This time the quiet continued and Father John's concern for Judy grew.

"Judy, what is troubling you?"

She wrung her hands without an answer.

"Are you sick?"

"Are you on drugs?" Judy nodded affirmatively.

"What drug?"

Judy replied, "Speed," wringing her hands again and putting her head down and to the side. Then Judy said, "I'm here to get away from it."

The padre felt anger at meeting the demon of drugs again. He knew he could do nothing and he fought to accept his own powerlessness.

Years of prison ministry had taught Father John that only the addict could excise the evil of drugs. Those who tried to help were often pulled down like a would-be rescuer trying to save a drowning swimmer. Those closest to an addict often had to rebuild their own lives like so many ruined buildings left in the swath of a hurricane. The demon of drugs swirled, absorbing the time and energy of the padre now as it had so many well-meaning people in Judy's life before.

"Are you traveling with anyone?"

"No. I left my daughters with my mom in San Diego."

The soft brown eyes of the priest turned hard and black when he learned Judy had children. He tensed for a moment and only gradually returned to normal.

"I tried to hurt myself. I'm afraid," Judy whined.

Red lights flashed like sirens in Father John's mind as hot words flared from his mouth,

"Your life is not your own. It belongs to God! Think of your daughters!"

Judy searched her backpack for a wadded up tissue and dabbed her red, puffy eyes.

"How long have you been on speed?"

"Eight, ahh, maybe nine years."

"Have you ever tried to stop before?"

"Yes," Judy said with quivering lips.

"Why should this time be any different?" the priest asked with an interrogating tone. Judy recoiled at the question as if she had been struck to the heart.

"I don't know," she cried out. "I can't go on."

Judy thought she wanted to stop using the drug because she felt miserable. She also vaguely realized that, as her daughters grew older, she would have to make a choice between the speed and her children. Her maternal instincts told her she could not hide the habit any longer.

Father John could see the whites of Judy's eyes as they rolled back into her head.

"Judy, if you were left alone, do you think you would harm yourself?"

Judy squirmed in her seat feeling that she would not make it through the night alone. She answered for herself but didn't think to respond to the priest. Father John asked again, with a louder voice,

"Judy, are you thinking of hurting yourself?"

"Yes," she mumbled softly.

"Judy, I would like to take you to the hospital. They can treat you as you come off the drug. I don't know how," the priest confessed. "Would that be acceptable?"

Judy nodded affirmatively and smiled a little, much to the relief of Father John.

"Good decision, Judy."

Father John stood tall and led Judy out of the office to his golf cart, the most common form of transportation on the island. The electrical cart quietly left St. Catherine's and turned uphill on a road leading inland that passed the fire station. The smell of sage mixed with a cloud of dust as the small wheels merged onto Avalon Canyon Road. Halting in front of the hospital, Father John helped Judy to her feet and opened the door to the emergency room for her.

The staff of the municipal hospital proudly professed to work at a facility that remained open twenty-four/seven. Equipped to deliver any acute care, the doctors and nurses mostly occupied themselves with dispensing antibiotics and bandaging bloody toes.

"Hi, Father John! What brings you here this fine evening? Do you have an earache? I thought you'd be at the jazz festival," a nurse said, emphasizing the word "ear" as if she knew things about him to which only his doctor was privy.

"Good evening, Connie," Father John said as Judy stepped out from behind him and stood in front of the reception window. Connie's cheerful demeanor turned professional. The padre leaned over and asked Judy,

"Can I tell her what the problem is?" Judy nodded affirmatively. Then the priest whispered to Connie,

"She is suicidal and is coming off speed. Her name is Judy." The nurse clasped a large metallic clipboard with reams of paper attached. Her dexterous fingers scanned for the appropriate policy and procedure. Then she handed Father John a form. Once Judy supplied her contact information and insurance card they were instructed to sit down.

"How long will it be?" Father John asked.

"Not long," the nurse replied. This time Judy remained calm and the padre fidgeted. The two sat quietly.

"I'm cold," Judy said.

The paternal instinct in the padre took over and he asked the nurse for a blanket with a slightly demanding voice as if to say, "Can't you see she's freezing?" The nurse left her post. Father John rubbed his palms together as if to warm himself. The nurse returned with a folded pink blanket.

"Thank you, Connie," Father John said in a voice that expressed gratitude and sought forgiveness. Judy had her arms crossed. Then, seeing the priest walk toward her, she leaned forward in her seat. Father John opened the blanket and gently placed it over Judy's shoulders. She smiled warmly and held the soft blanket close to herself. The padre felt love and affection for Judy.

A few minutes later Connie came for Judy. Father John stood tall, more alive than ever, saying,

"You will be in my prayer tonight. You'll be just fine. They will take good care of you and I hope to see you at church tomorrow." Judy looked up at the priest and nodded. Connie took Judy's hand and placed an arm around her blanketed shoulders and led her away.

Father John walked out of the sterile hospital into the vibrant evening. The narrow canyon reverberated with the croaking of frogs and the chirping of crickets. A Rain Bird sprinkler clicked through its cycle and the padre could smell the dew-covered grass. He took a deep breath as he sat in the golf cart. Then he sped down Catalina Avenue.

Turning onto Crescent Avenue bound for Casino Way, the padre heard jazz bouncing among the Avalon hills. The island visitors buzzed and boats swayed to the festive atmosphere. Strangers greeted each other like old friends with a wave of happiness and a shared sense of contentment.

The padre arrived at The Casino and picked his way along the steep interior ramp amid an exuberant maze of glamorous gowns and snappy silk trousers. Hundreds of Cinderellas with their princes moved over a cork-covered, hardwood dance floor under the soaring ribbed ceiling of the 20,000 square-foot ballroom. A waitress carried an opal inlaid tray with green olives suspended from the stems of Martini glasses. A saxophone erupted from the stage and charmed the listeners to a perfect island night.

Father John, looking over the crowd like a search light, couldn't find his friends. Then he remembered the Harmonds advertising their table as a *high topper* with a direct line of sight to the stage. The padre moved to the elevated seating and spotted his friends, who were absorbed in the music. When the padre arrived, they stood to greet him with an embrace.

"You made it! Can I get you a drink?"

"Yes, I made it, and it looks like I'm just in time," the padre replied with a smile as he looked at some spilled gin on the white table cloth.

"Who's playing tonight?"

"*Pieces of a Dream* and *Soul Ballet*."

The padre sat down with a laugh and asked,

"Did you say *Pieces of a Dream* and *Soul Ballet*?"

"Yep, you heard me right. Crazy, huh? You have to remember, it's soft jazz in the summer groove," his friend joked.

Father John marveled at the band names as he retraced the strides of his own soul from a bed of pain and shattered dreams to a ballroom of joy.

"I'll have a drink."

The nurse had supplied Judy with a mild sedative as she lay on the white sheet gurney in the emergency room. Connie's light cheer and heavy concern endeared her to the patient.

Judy remembered not this evening but a dark night years ago. She was at a Hollywood club smoking crystal meth for the first time. Judy wanted to forget the memory like a woman trying to break off a relationship with a stalker who keeps recalling the first date.

Judy, a high school junior, partied with her senior girlfriends. A stretch limo picked them up carrying a drug with a promise to keep them dancing all night. One of the graduates burned ice with a lighter and it melted in Judy's brain. Her mood and body movement were seemingly enhanced for a night. Her brain was damaged like a smashed pumpkin for life.

One of Judy's friends stole the drug from her older brother, a drug dealer. He purchased the meth from a motorcycle gang. A Hell's Angel bought the drug from a warehouse in Long Beach. The warehouse distribution center was supplied by trucks that crossed the border into the United States from Mexico.

The piece of crystal meth smoked by Judy crossed the border and arrived at the warehouse in a dilapidated, leaky, blue refrigeration truck with shiny, new metallic signs on the doors. The logo consisted of the red letter and number "F3" below a picture of a blue fish that flashed like new chrome wheels on a rusty old car.

Chapter Nineteen
Wind Shift

Precise Intuition ran down wind toward Hen Rock just off Catalina Island. The wind whispered calmly over the placid Pacific waters. The red "F3" logo and blue fish print on the spinnaker sail hung limply.

"Prepare to douse the spinnaker," Martin called out.

Andrew, the youngest, finished counting every winged creature not only with his fingers but also with his toes.

"I counted twenty-eight birds and bugs."

"Good," Vanessa said with an affirming tone she reserved only for her youngest. "Come back here with me." She wanted Isaac and Andrew near her in the stern and out of harm's way for the impending take-down of the sail. Martin stood next to Luke at the mast and briefed him on the maneuver with the instructions,

"You stand here and lower the halyard."

"This one, dad?" Luke asked as he tugged on a rope.

"Yes, that's the one, son. In this light air you can let it down fairly fast, but not too fast. Listen to me. If I say slow down, slow down, so the sail doesn't fall into the water."

Martin let the guy run free and started gathering in the foot of the spinnaker. Soon colorful cloth filled his arms. After a few minutes, the sail was stowed neatly below and the spinnaker pole fastened safely away.

Precise Intuition sailed on, now less than a nautical mile from her anchorage. Martin made a mental fix of the boat's position after identifying Long Point and Moonstone Cove.

"Dad, can I bring up the sextant yet?" Luke pleaded.

Martin promised his oldest son earlier in the day that they would take the sensitive instrument, used for celestial navigation, out of its case and familiarize themselves with its use.

"One thing at a time," Martin said. He concentrated on where and how they would anchor the boat. "Let's bring in the jib first and take down the main. Once we are safely anchored to the land, we'll set our sights on the sky."

"It's not even dark yet," Isaac said with a shrug of his shoulders.

The crew of *Precise Intuition* busied itself with the duties that occupy a ship as it prepares to make harbor. The sails were fastened, the anchor readied and the engine started. The boat swept along the bay and came to rest above a sandy bottom in five fathoms of water. Martin turned the bow in the direction he thought the next breeze might blow.

"Down anchor," Martin ordered. Vanessa, standing on the bow, lowered the anchor over the side as the boat slowly drifted backward. Vanessa cleatted off the anchor line marked for depth after three hundred feet. Martin placed the gears in reverse and throttled slightly as he checked the vessel's movement against a few stationary boulders. Confident of the anchor's firm hold, and confirming his observation with a question to Vanessa, he killed the engine.

Precise Intuition floated gently in place about a hundred yards off the rocky shore. Martin and Vanessa's movements on-board slowed comfortably into relaxation as smiles of contentment settled over their faces. They savored the beauty of a contemplative moment.

The boys became anxious in the silent inactivity. Soon they started fidgeting. Luke flicked the brass hinge on the wooden container that housed the sextant. Isaac banged through the fishing lures in his plastic tackle box. Andrew, fingers and toes spread wide, scampered along the deck searching for bugs to count. Soon the cacophony of flicking, banging, and scampering turned into giggles.

Martin yearned to take his daily swim even as his promise about preparations for the evening star observations beckoned. He felt insecure about trying to teach his son something he had not mastered himself. Martin prepared to notify Luke about postponing the removal of the sextant from its wooden case when Andrew proclaimed,

"There's the moon." No sooner did the words leave Andrew's mouth when the brass hinge on the wooden case opened and the velvet sock protecting the sextant fell away. The half-lit waxing moon was twelve days old; the time elapsed since the new moon.

"Not so fast," Martin said, needing to refresh his own memory. "First let's review our astronomy." Luke complied slowly, turning the sextant over in his hands, careful not to touch the optical lenses of the telescope, mirrors or glass before setting it home.

"First," addressing the whole family, Martin asked, "looking at the celestial sphere, can anyone spot Venus?" Luke spotted the evening star, the name given to Venus because it rises within about three hours of sunset. The misnomer given to the planet also applies at sunrise when it is called the morning star.

"There it is," Luke pointed, with some impatience.

"Good," Martin responded. "Now, how do we determine what other celestial bodies we can use for navigational purposes this evening?"

"We can use the star chart for the autumn sky," Luke answered.

"Very good," Vanessa said as Isaac and Andrew listened to the escalating difficulty of the quiz being administered to their older brother.

"Can you get the chart for us?" Martin asked.

"Yes," Luke said with a more heartened response. Returning with the star chart, Luke handed it to his dad. The family gathered around the teak table in the cockpit and unfolded the heavenly map.

"It's a clear day so tonight we should be able to see Pegasus." Before Martin could say anything more, Andrew started flapping his arms like wings and galloped in place, yelling,

"Pegasus, Pegasus, Pegasus."

"Sit down already," Isaac said on behalf of the crew.

"Who can tell me which navigational stars are found within the constellation Pegasus?"

"Enif and Mar... Mar," Luke replied hesitantly.

"Markab," Martin said as he studied the chart, impressed with his son's grasp of the autumn sky. "At dusk we will look for Markab and Alphratz with the star finder. We might even use the star Diphda in the constellation Cetus, meaning sea monster, or Hamal in Aries, the ram," Martin concluded.

One of the things that attracted Martin to sailing and kept his interest was the closeness he felt to the elements, tides and seasons. In his rapidly changing life he took solace in those phenomena that change, but with some constancy and predictability. He looked forward to watching the slow wheeling constellations move across the still heavens.

The boys felt their father's anticipation with excitement.

"Because of the regularity of the universe," Martin said soberly, "and because long ago astronomers, our forefathers, began keeping track of the motions of the celestial bodies, we can predict their location relative to the earth at any given instant."

"Star gazing also inspired the calendar," Vanessa added. "Nearly two thousand five hundred years ago the Maya had a 260 day calendar. Some say it was derived from the amount of time between solar zenith passages near the equator. Others say the 260 days are based on the human life cycle and the length of gestation."

"Gestation?" Andrew repeated comically, not knowing the significance of the word.

"The time you were in the oven," Martin answered. Andrew replied with a blank stare.

"The amount of time we were in mom's belly before being born," Luke said.

"260 days is the usual time from the first missed menstrual flow of blood to birth," Vanessa said authoritatively.

"Mom, that's more than we need to know," Luke said.

"Can we get back to the navigation now?" Martin asked.

"I didn't want you guys to miss women's contribution to all of this!" Martin, raising his eyebrows, acknowledged Vanessa. Then he talked about the celestial triangle used for navigation and the trigonometry that underlies its use.

"Is that like bringing the star or planets down with the sextant?" Luke asked.

"Not quite. We use the sextant to make precise measurements of the angle between two lines of sight from the observer. We take one to the celestial body and the other to the horizon. With the help of a few tables we bring the observations down to our chart to obtain a star fix and our almost exact location."

158

Martin's speech betrayed him. His use of the sextant was only theoretical, not yet based on experiential knowledge. In fact, Martin began to think the sextant was for long journeys around the world, not a few days cruising Catalina.

"Oh," Luke responded. After a few seconds he rejoined,

"Maybe the Maya brought down their own triangle from the celestial sphere and planted it on the earth in the form of the pyramids."

Vanessa and Martin looked at each other, amazed at their son's precociousness.

"I think the pyramids were constructed with reference to the equinoxes," Martin answered in a speculative voice as he placed his arm around the broadening shoulders of Luke. Andrew, suddenly and completely bored with the topic, asked his mom,

"Will we see the rabbit tonight?

"The rabbit?" Andrew asked.

"The rabbit on the moon," Isaac added.

"Not tonight," Vanessa replied. "It is not a full moon." An invisible wind swirled through her black hair. Then Vanessa started sharing a Mesoamerican creation story.

"Long, long ago, the sun and moon shone with the same intensity. They came into existence when two brave and generous gods threw themselves into a fire. One of the gods, the sun, struck the face of the other god with a rabbit, transforming him into the moon. From that time on the silhouette of a rabbit could be seen on the face of the moon. But at that time, the sun and moon still occupied the same place in the sky and did not move. Then the god of wind blew, separating the two gods and setting the sun and the moon on their paths.

"The earth was in darkness until the gods sacrificed themselves in the fire. To prepare for this they did penance and offered quetzal feathers, gold, thorns of jade, dried leaves, cane, pine needles and their bloody wounds. After their pilgrimage up the mountain and their penance, they threw themselves into the flame. That is why the sun is blood red at its setting."

As Vanessa finished the story, the children huddled around their parents while the wind blew in and the sun set behind the mountainous island.

"I know why the sun and moon appear reddish-orange," Luke said confidently with the science to dissipate the legend.

"When the sun and moon are near the horizon their light must pass through more of the atmosphere than when they are directly overhead. This larger amount of atmosphere only allows a small amount of the blue light to reach us, leaving only the long-wavelength red light."

"Smarty," Vanessa said, well aware of the natural explanation. Then she continued to talk about the beliefs of the indigenous people of Mexico.

"I told you about the 260-day calendar but the Mesoamericans also had a 360-day calendar. When the two were set in motion it took 52 years, or a calendar round, for a given day to reoccur. The Aztecs held a fire ceremony at its completion. The days before the end of the round were dangerous, for during those days the gods might decide to end life on earth. At midnight, before the first day of the year, a sacrificial victim, prepared well in advance, was brought to the altar, maybe on top of one of the pyramids. Then his chest was cut open and his heart removed. There, in his open chest, a flame was started. The new flame assured a new day with the light from the morning sun and the opening of another 52-year cycle."

"Honey, I think you're scaring the kids," Martin said as Andrew's fingers dug into his arm.

"We're not scared," Isaac retorted. Andrew, for his part, had heard enough. He found it easier to imagine winged horses and count the fire flies and blue green beetles that might have ridden the winds north from Mazatlán to Catalina. However, after the stories his mom told, he wasn't about to leave his dad's side.

"If the gods sacrificed themselves to bring light, why should it surprise us that people sacrificed one another to keep the light burning and to prevent a collision between the heavens and the earth?" Vanessa mused, trying to understand for herself the primitive impulses of her ancestors.

Isaac began to cry.

"It might have been nobler if the victims had gone willingly," Martin replied with a sigh.

"Don't we strive to imitate Christ, the Light of the World? Did he not willingly lay down his life for his friends? Jesus never took life but restores life, bringing us to the fullness of life," Vanessa reflected.

Isaac tried to wipe the tears from his eyes. Vanessa saw a drop fall and reached to hug him. Isaac turned away with folded arms. Vanessa stood and embraced him.

"You're not going to sacrifice us are you?" Isaac asked, looking up at his mother with sobs.

"I love you. We're not going to let anything happen to you." Isaac placed his face upon his mother's bosom as she caressed his head and turned to the one thing that calmed her children when they were anxious or afraid: prayer. Taking after her father Raul, Vanessa had learned a few psalms by heart. She gently spoke some of the words of Psalm Eight into the ear of her upset son.

> How great is your name, O Lord our God, through all the earth!...When I see the heavens, the work of your hands, the moon and the stars which you arranged... why do you care about us?...Yet you have made us little less than a god; with glory and honor you crown us, you give us

power over the works of your hand, put all things under our feet...All of them...birds of the air, and fish that make their way through the waters...How great is your name, O Lord our God, through all the earth!

"How great is your name, O Lord our God, through all the earth," Isaac repeated in a duet of praise. Then Vanessa proclaimed another biblical verse from the Book of Revelation.

A great sign appeared in the sky, a woman clothed with the sun, with the moon under her feet, and on her head a crown of twelve stars.

Vanessa's lips moved in a gentle voice as she prayed a *Hail Mary* with Isaac. The boy stopped crying and sat down with his mother. Andrew, who often approached his brother only to hit him and then run, sat at his side, so as to comfort him, and stayed awhile. Martin, encircled by his sons, recalled an event from his childhood.

"I remember a night I spent on the beach south of Mazatlán when I was a boy. I awoke in the middle of the night. There were more points of light than darkness in the sky. I watched the waves approach the shore under the starlight and listened to them echo through the night. I suddenly saw a bright orange streak move along the horizon. I had time to wonder what it meant as I watched in awe."

"It sounds like a comet," Luke said melodramatically.

"Maybe you're right," Martin responded.

"Dad, it looks like there are still a few hours of daylight left. Can I take the zodiac out and go fishing?"

"I wanta go; I wanta go," Isaac added.

Martin looked out over the water. He saw a few cat's paws farther out at sea where a west wind blew weakly but more consistently. The sailboat had rotated around the anchor to meet the wind head on as it lined up parallel to the shore.

"Yes, you can take the dingy out, but take your brother. You can make preparations now while I take my swim. Give me your float plan when I return."

"Yeah!" Luke exclaimed. "Put the tackle boxes into the boat," Luke commanded Isaac as he pointed at the plastic containers filled with metal fishing lures.

Martin went down below to the cabin and changed into his bathing suit and grabbed a towel and his swim goggles. Vanessa encouraged the boys to drink some water and shared a bottle with Andrew.

Returning to the deck, Martin warmed up for his swim with all the ceremony of an Acapulco cliff diver. Martin rotated his head, shook his arms and legs in turn, took a few deep breaths and climbed the bow pulpit, steadying himself for the dive off *Precise Intuition*.

Martin's quick jump in the air and sleek plunge in the water made a small splash that reverberated through the serene bay.

The boys peered over the side of the boat following their dad's progress through the clear water. Martin came up for air, waved, took a breath, and then headed for the depths. As he swam under the keel Vanessa and the boys moved from one side of the boat to the other. When Martin resurfaced, his family sighed with relief.

Diving again, Martin headed for the anchor line and stayed with it all the way to the bottom, thirty-five feet below, stopping to equalize with the changes in atmosphere. Satisfied with the hold of the Danforth anchor and with lungs beginning to ache, Martin pushed off the sandy bottom and rose to the surface with a few exhaled bubbles.

After another wave to his family Martin swam away from the boat toward shore in a steady freestyle cadence. He checked his respiration and felt his heart pumping in his chest. His biceps and hamstrings stretched to the stroke. As Martin approached the shore and the shallower water he startled a bat ray that returned the favor. He increased his speed to keep up with the graceful flight of the fish that soon disappeared from his vision. Martin took a mental inventory of his body, relaxed, and continued to swim in a path parallel to the rocky shore.

Drawing close to some submerged boulders, Martin felt the tidal surge sweep him from side to side as he reached and kicked forward. He enjoyed the feeling of water moving over his body and thought to himself, "This is great!"

Most of Martin's swims were motivated by compulsion, not pleasure.

Martin stopped swimming to watch aquamarine wave shadows roll over the textured valleys on the sandy white bottom. The blue water magnified his wonder as the breathing green vibrancy of life pulsed with yellow-light joy.

A patch of kelp floated nearby and offshore a bit. The golden shape on the blue sea made for an inviting destination. Martin altered his course and soon reached the bubble-leafed sea plant. The kelp forest was so thick and buoyant Martin lay on top of it like a raft. He looked into the sky, and then rotating with the help of his hands and feet, passed some time gazing up at the cliffs.

Back on the sailboat, Vanessa, who used to worry for Martin's safety during his ocean swims, read a novel. Isaac sat in the dingy with the tackle boxes asking his brother,

"Can we go? Let's go." Vanessa overheard him and responded,

"Not until your father gets back."

"Where is he?" Luke asked Andrew.

"Over there, see; he's coming toward us now."

The current pushed Martin speedily forward through the sea. He reached the stern of the boat and yelled,

"Luke, put the swim ladder down for me."

Luke let the ladder swing down into the water and Martin climbed aboard *Precise Intuition*.

"That was great! I saw a bat ray and a few big fish too." Martin also described some red, orange and purple starfish that clung to the underwater sides of the barnacled boulders. "There must be some good tide pools along that shoreline for exploring."

Indeed, Hermit crabs wandered across the pools like planets along the solar system. Dark, rocky crevices channeled living water in and out of the rippled tide pools like stellar winds and the gravitational force of black holes pushing and pulling the elements across space. And just waiting to be discovered, like the observation of the outer reaches of a constellation, an octopus pulsed in all its large eyed, tentacled, chameleon majesty.

"Andrew, how about looking for shells in the tide pools tomorrow?" Martin asked. "We will stand in the silky green eel grass as hermit crabs crawl along our arms." Andrew remained speechless but a seal barked its approval and clapped its flippers in the distance.

"Cool," Luke said. "Can we go now?"

"Let me dry off first and then tell me where you plan on going," Martin said as he dried his hair and patted his chest with a towel. Martin thought about a change of clothes and the nap that awaited him, but he first needed to hear Luke's plan and check the condition of his craft as the wind increased.

The winds had been strange but not uncommon for late summer, early autumn in Catalina. A southeasterly blew under ten knots much of the day, only to be confronted by the prevailing west by northwest wind later. Where the two winds met, the air stayed still and the water remained flat. But as the prevailing winds grew in strength and the easterly died, the complexion of the sea changed. Just off Long Point, free from the footprint of the island and exposed to the west, whitecaps had formed.

The bay, however, appeared calm to Martin, just rippled in a few places, but safe for a dingy and his two sons. So he thought, as Luke approached with his long-billed hat.

"Tell me what you have in mind, son?"

"It's pretty simple, dad. We're just going to paddle over to those rocks and catch some fish. How far can we go without a motor anyway?"

Martin stood up and checked the dingy that floated a few feet aft on the port side of *Precise Intuition*.

"Are both oars on board and life jackets for each of you?"

"Yes, they are in there, dad." Martin confirmed the response with a visual inspection of his own.

"Good. Just stay along the shore line and be back in an hour."

"Okay, dad," Luke replied as he said, "Let's go!" to his brother Isaac.

Luke stepped off the stern, down the swim ladder and sat in the middle of the dingy first. Isaac followed and sat on the other side until Luke ordered him to take a seat up front. Martin uncleated the line and threw it to the eight-foot dingy. Luke fastened both oars into place and began paddling for shore. Martin, Vanessa and Andrew watched until the raft arrived at an outcropping of rocks and the boys began to fish.

Vanessa placed a sweater on Andrew who fell asleep at her side. Then she started reading her novel again. After seeing his son off and viewing the first cast, Martin lay down, closed his eyes, and remembered the last day he had seen his dad on the beach in Mazatlán.

Meanwhile, after a few casts with different lures and no bites, Luke prepared to try another spot. He rowed close to shore and skirted a reef.

"I just know there are some yellowtail in that kelp," Luke said to his brother.

"What lure should I use?" Isaac asked.

"Try that purple spoon and I'll use this red one."

Isaac tied his knot as Luke lined up for his cast. The sparkling lure whizzed high in the air and landed just where Luke aimed. The spin of the reel matched his vital pulse. Luke turned the handle quickly. Suddenly the sensitive rod bent down with the pull of the line.

"I've got a bite," Luke said excitingly. Isaac hurried to finish his knot so he could make a cast and get in on the action.

"Wait. Don't cast now, you'll tangle the lines," Luke yelled with excitement. "Get the net!"

"What is it, can you see it?" Isaac asked. The fish pulled the little dingy further out into the bay, so Luke ordered,

"Fasten the oars and put them in the water. Maybe it will slow the fish down."

"Luke, what is it?"

"I think it is a yellowtail," Luke replied tentatively. Then Luke spotted a silver streak slicing through the water.

"It's a barracuda. I think I can land it but watch out for the teeth. Dad says they're sharp."

The rod moved up and down and Luke struggled to take line against the fish. Then, just as suddenly as the fish took the bait, the sharp teeth of the barracuda sawed off the fishing line.

"Ohhhh!" Luke moaned. "I lost him." Isaac did not waste any time empathizing. With the excitement of the first bite, he made a cast toward shore.

"I've got something," Isaac exclaimed.

"You caught a rock or piece of sea weed," Luke said after watching the line. "It's a snag."

The two brothers worked together to loosen the snag. Andrew pulled and Luke paddled closer to the reef. They retrieved the lure and rested in the dingy for a moment.

Then Luke studied Long Point. He formulated a plan for staying close to shore but one that would allow him and his brother to move farther out to sea where he thought the bigger fish were.

"Let's paddle along this beach and then along that point. Look at all those reefs and kelp. I know there will be some yellowtail or sea bass in there."

"No, I wanna go back," Isaac wined.

"Why? It's not that far. I'll do the paddling and let you make the first cast."

"Okay," Isaac replied, feeling nervous so far from *Precise Intuition*.

The current carried the little craft along the shoreline and farther from the beaches in the bay. The current gave Luke a false sense of confidence in his rowing. The dingy had not yet reached Pirate's Cove, the inlet just before the tip of Long Point, when the breeze freshened and the seas began to rise. With all their attention focused on fishing, the brothers did not perceive the dangerous conditions brewing just around the corner.

Chapter Twenty
Israel's Anniversary Gift in Ensenada

"Come out here, darling. I've got a surprise for you," Claudia said from the porch of her and her husband's lavish suite on the upper deck of a cruise ship in the bay of *Todos Santos*.

"Look, pictures of our wedding. I found them a few weeks ago and was saving them for today." Claudia handed Israel the first picture, a close up of the bridesmaid and best man. Martin in a tuxedo and Vanessa in a blue dress smiled for the camera as they stood in front of the First Methodist Church.

"Ten years already," Israel said. "How are they?"

"I spoke to Vanessa a couple of months ago. They all sound fine. You should call him," Claudia said, passing the next picture, the cutting of a four-tiered wedding cake at Raul's Place.

"I still remember the first night we met," Claudia said as she looked over the ocean, glanced at Israel, and turned back toward the sea. "It was a Halloween party at Raul's Place. I was the only one wearing a costume. A week later you called inviting me to a play. Vanessa tried to get me to break the date."

Claudia handed Israel the next photograph, a picture of him placing the ring on her finger, and said,

"We saw *The Man of La Mancha*. We went out a few more times and then you didn't call for almost a year. I thought you lost interest."

Claudia waited for a reply from Israel, who stood quietly next to her flipping back to the picture of Martin and Vanessa. Passing another photo, one of her parents, Claudia said,

"When you did call again, you wanted to get married. Vanessa couldn't believe that you proposed and with only a three month engagement. She said you did it for the citizenship."

"It was time to be married," Israel replied, holding his hand out nonchalantly for the next picture. "And Vanessa, one moment she's against us, and the next she is your bridesmaid at our wedding."

"How come, after ten years, it still doesn't feel like we've settled down?" Claudia asked as she looked up from the blinding reflection on the water into Israel's shaded hazel eyes.

"It has been ten years and you have always known work and travel are a part of my life," Israel grumbled as he handed the stack of pictures back to Claudia and moved to leave her side and return to the suite.

"Will you put some lotion on my back?"

Claudia, a petite, small-boned woman, handed Israel the tanning lotion and untied her bikini top. Her cup-D-sized breasts dangled in front of Israel. The sight of Claudia's breast augmentation reminded Israel of his vasectomy, even though the surgeries took place so many years before. Claudia's artificial enhancement occurred just months after his procedure.

Israel took the tanning lotion and rubbed it onto Claudia's fair and rounded skin. With Claudia glistening in the sun, Israel turned back for the room again.

"Where are you going? Sit out in the sun with me."

"I need to get dressed and go to town," Israel responded.

"It's our anniversary. Stay here with me."

"We have been together for the last couple of days. I need to check on business and visit Eduardo. He has an anniversary present for us."

"Why doesn't he come visit us here on the ship?"

"He can't do that. And no, I won't have you go up there," Israel said as he looked over Esenada and up the coastal mountains to *Bellavista*. "You sure you don't want to have dinner in town tonight? Maybe he could join us and present his gift to both of us?"

"No. It's champagne and room service tonight," Claudia said as she stood and looked into Israel's placid hazel eyes.

"I need to go," Israel said mechanically. "What are you doing today?"

"Aerobic class, day spa, a massage and shopping."

"Good. I'll return around five," Israel said as he entered the room and put on a pair of slacks, a dress shirt and a sport coat. Soon he boarded a ferry for shore and hailed a cab.

The drive up Mexico Highway One brought back memories of Martin and Jose and the leaky blue truck. When the cab dropped Israel off in El Sauzal, he looked at the fishing boats nostalgically to see if the *St. Augustine* was in, even though he knew Jose and his crew followed the fish farther south five years before.

Fresh, Fish, Fast grew side by side with Israel's business and just as rapidly. Though Israel never spoke about nor in any way affiliated himself with his old friends after he went into partnership with *La Tortuga*, he followed their success. He was most pleased when Jose purchased the *St. Augustine* from the retiring Luigi.

Israel walked away from the waterfront. He passed by the old warehouse and entered a new office building where he searched for his local supervisor. When he found the supervisor, he secured a private office with a phone. Two clerks brought in stacks of computer reports with the status and location of all the Escobin Cartel's moving assets, an area that covered all of north-western Mexico and the southwestern United States.

Israel, actively in charge of distribution for the cartel's legal and illegal businesses, studied the maintenance schedule for three planes and considered the purchase of a fourth. He called on the status of a delayed shipment and expressed his regrets to the customer. After two and a half hours and a few more phone calls, Israel studied the statistics Eduardo always inquired about and left the office.

Carlos waited outside by his sports car in his designated parking space, blowing and rubbing the rings on his fat fingers to a dull polish, until he saw Israel approach. He opened the door for Israel and then drove him south on Highway One and through the gate at Eduardo Escobin's compound in *Bellavista*.

Eduardo was as slow to greet Israel as a turtle venturing out of his shell. Only after Israel was ushered by the guards holding AK-47s did Eduardo meet him saying,

"Happy anniversary, Israel," as they walked to the room overlooking the bay.

"Carlos, bring us some Tequila and take Israel's coat." Carlos removed Israel's coat and opened the door leading to the balcony. Eduardo and Israel walked out onto the veranda and watched the activity around the cruise ship in the bay of *Todos Santos*. Eduardo smiled with cunning eyes over his beaked nose and said through tight lips,

"Let's go inside for our drinks; it's too bright out here."

The two men sat close to each other in a pair of ornately gilded French Provincial chairs.

"Are you enjoying the cruise?"

"Yes. I'm eating at the cafés one moment and jogging on the track the next. Last night we danced at the nightclub for the first time in years."

Eduardo lifted two shot glasses, partially filled with tequila that had been poured over ice, from a silver tray and handed one to Israel. After a swallow, Eduardo asked,

"How many days have you been at sea?"

"This is the fourth day," Israel responded after a sip, holding the glass in his hand. "While I've been cruising, your trains, planes and trucks keep moving." Israel set the drink on a coaster and methodically reported statistics on operating costs and tons of cargo shipped for each segment of the Escobin Cartel's business. He concluded with hesitation by saying,

"Our on-time percentage was 93% for the week."

"The number will be up by the end of the month. You work too much. Today is your anniversary. Enough business," Eduardo said with a wide grin that left Israel tipping his glass of tequila.

"I have an anniversary gift. Carlos, bring that box to Israel. You can open it later with Claudia."

Israel accepted the neatly gift-wrapped box.

"Now, I have a surprise for you," Eduardo said.

Israel set down his empty drink, the glass bottom magnifying the serpent and claws grasping human hearts on a coaster depicting The Calendar Stone.

"Let's go downstairs," Eduardo said as he stood up. Israel followed and reached for his coat that lay over the back of a leather couch.

"You won't need that," Eduardo said as they left the room and walked down two flights of stairs to the bottom floor of the compound.

Eduardo and Carlos stopped in front of a door that Israel recognized. He identified it as the entrance to the windowless room he had been taken to the first time he was brought to *Bellavista*, though he had reached it by a different route. Carlos took a stainless steel key from his pocket and fit it into a lock. Eduardo looked on with a wide grin. The hinges of the door spread with the expression on Eduardo's face.

"Surprise."

Orlando Melendez's swollen eyes peered up with instant fright from deep black and blue sockets. He sat in one of the room's two metal chairs, skinny and pale with his hands tied behind his back, a bloodied shirt, without shoes.

Initially stunned by the sight of his brother's assailant, Israel began to feel anger that tightened his gut like a drum and made his heart beat loudly in his chest. A sense of power surged through Israel as he looked at Eduardo, then at Orlando, and back at Eduardo.

"He's all yours, partner."

"Carlos, stand him up for me," Israel said. Carlos looked at Eduardo who nodded and used the intercom to call for help. After another man arrived and set down his gun, Orlando was untied and lifted out of his seat and held, his knees too wobbly to stand on his own.

Israel's green eyes glared. He reeled back with his right hand in a fist and punched Orlando in the stomach with all his might. Orlando's head and shoulders dropped with the impact. Orlando heaved to catch his breath as the artificial light droned on.

"That's for me. What shall we do about my brother?"

Israel looked around the room and noticed, for the first time, instruments of torture. Eduardo watched with a sadistic grin that stoked the fire of Israel's anger. But within Israel, stemming the tide of his hate like a giant rock set in a raging river, was an element, a memory, that he couldn't name. He took a deep breath, looked at Carlos and Eduardo, and paced around the small room. The florescent bulbs droned. Then Israel recalled the vow he had made to the priest with his father on the day of Joaquin's death.

Meanwhile, Eduardo and Carlos glanced at each other.

"This side of the business is new to you," Eduardo said.

"Let me make a suggestion or show you? Beginners often do the work too fast."

"No, no. Just give me a moment. Carlos, sit him down and tie him back up," Israel demanded with a wavering voice as he resumed his introspective pacing around the small room.

Carlos picked up a pair of tweezers and an instrument that resembled an ice-pick and sharpened one against the other. Orlando began to moan.

Israel stopped his pacing and stood in front of the captive. He reeled back again, this time with an open hand, and slapped Orlando with all his strength.

"That is enough for now," Israel said. Then he looked at Eduardo, indicating he wanted out of the room. The door shut on Orlando's sobbing. Carlos turned the key to lock the door.

"Can we speak about this upstairs?" Israel asked.

When Eduardo reached the top of the stairs and the room overlooking the bay, he said,

"Carlos, wait for us downstairs."

Eduardo, with some agitation, motioned for Israel to sit down as he stood behind him.

"I hand you the killer of your own brother. He's downstairs, within your power, and you want to talk about it?" Eduardo grunted.

"Where did you get him?"

"He was trying to move some cocaine over the border in Tijuana."

"You know he is Melendez's son?"

"Of course. Are you worried about him? You should be more concerned about me."

"Eduardo," Israel pleaded. "There is one thing I want more than the death of my brother's killer. I want his father's land in *Jalisco*. He doesn't live there. You said Orlando was all mine and I would like to exchange him for the land," Israel proposed.

"What was he doing in my territory?"

Israel thought for a moment, moving his hand through his still black but thinning hair and said,

"If he entered your territory on his own, without his father's knowledge, we make the exchange and receive assurances that he works with you to see that your boundaries are respected. If he went at his father's bidding ..."

"Do I have the luxury of such leniency?" Eduardo asked loudly.

"With all due respect, if Orlando is here on his own, you gain an ally."

Eduardo took Israel's hand and gestured for him to stand up with a polite smile that took the place of the sadistic grin on his face.

"If that is what you want, I'll make some inquiries and consider it. Now, why don't you go to your wife. Call me when you return from your cruise."

Israel picked up his coat and the neatly wrapped gift for Claudia as Eduardo yelled for Carlos.

Chapter Twenty-One
Catalina Island Rescue

A bald eagle flew over the Isthmus at Catalina Island. With a dip of its wing, it soared East with a strong tail wind. The bird's golden eyes searched the rugged coast. The chrome bow pulpit of *Precise Intuition* shimmered over the blue-green water in a sheltered cove below. Within the wide arc of the hovering predator's pattern, a range that extended from Long Point to White's Landing and inland, two small boys floated in a dingy. The eagle started a dive, sharp talons unfolding. A long snake with a diamond shaped head and a rattle for a tail bathed in the heat of a dirt road near Echo Lake. The bird's claws pierced the thick reptilian scales in a cloud of dust.

The boys in the dingy, intent on catching fish, did not notice the bald eagle's flight over Long Point.

"You said I could go first!" Isaac reminded his brother. Luke bent down as Isaac cast his lure into the clear depths.

"Watch this cast," Luke said as he swung his rod back and forward in one motion. The lure splashed and sank, the reel clicked and spun.

"Look at the cave!" Isaac yelled with excitement as the dingy floated toward the end of Long Point. Luke glanced from his fishing line to the rocky opening with awe. Water roiled at the entrance and splashed in the dark recesses. Luke's hands felt for a bite as he peered as far into the cave as the light. The current continued carrying the boys in the shadow of the steep cliffs to a place where the boulders had slid into the sea. Here, too, the hard rocks had acquiesced to the persistent waves.

"There's a tunnel!" Isaac called out. The boys strained to see where its narrow incursion led. The tunnel went all the way through the point where a five-foot wind swell crashed in. Even starfish struggled to hang onto the slippery rocks and one another.

An open book lay face down on the deck in the cockpit of *Precise Intuition* at Vanessa's side. Andrew had his sweatered arms around his mother. Martin dreamt about his father in Mazatlán as the boat began to swing around its anchor.

The dingy was still hidden from the north westerly wind as it drifted through Pirates' Cove. Luke cast his lure near the end of Long Point and played the line. Isaac continued to watch the porous shore for caves and tunnels. Then the front of the dingy pitched. Luke tumbled backward in the shallow zodiac, falling into Isaac. The tips of the fishing rods pointed skyward. Luke pushed himself back up and gaped with surprise.

The turbulent sea rushed at the boys with a chaotic chop. Luke's eyes watered as he faced the wind. A gust caught the top of his long-billed cap and sent it flying.

"Take this," Luke said as he thrust his fishing rod at his brother and jumped over the side. Luke saw his hat on the surface of the water. He swam toward it slowly with his heavy tennis shoes. He clutched the hat in triumph and held it above his head like a trophy. When he turned back toward the dingy, it was gone.

The gust that blew Luke's cap off whistled through the halyards of *Precise Intuition*. Martin woke from his nap and sat up. He saw Andrew curled up near Vanessa in the seat across from him. Then he looked toward shore where he had last seen Luke and Isaac fishing. He followed the profile of the bay all the way to the light on top of Long Point.

A sinking feeling covered Luke until he heard his brother's scream. He kicked his legs to elevate above the swells and spotted the dingy. He made desperate strokes in the direction of Isaac's voice. He turned his head to take a breath and aspirated on a mouthful of saltwater. Coughing, he kicked again to raise himself above the chop.

"Help! Help!" Isaac screamed to his brother as he clutched the sides of the dingy. As the wind pushed the little boat farther out to sea, Isaac stopped yelling and started to cry. He crawled over the rods and tangled reels to the middle of the boat and reached for the oars. Setting the paddles in place, he began to row for the point. The oars splashed at the uneven chop futilely. Isaac kept trying to pull the unwieldy paddles until his hands blistered in frustration and his lungs burned with exhaustion. He let go of the oars and put on an orange life jacket.

"Honey! Honey!" Martin said as he nudged at Vanessa. "Where are the binoculars?"

"What?" Vanessa asked as she looked into Martin's blue-grey eyes.

"The binoculars. I was just looking for the boys. Are they back? I don't see the dingy," Martin asked.

"There they are," Vanessa responded, pointing at the binoculars and sitting up. Andrew was now awake in her lap. Martin began scanning the shore carefully, reached the end of Long Point, and looked out over the water.

"I don't see them," Martin said. He continued scanning the horizon. Then he saw a patch of orange against the twilight sky. Looking through the binoculars again, he saw Isaac in his life vest.

"Where's Luke?" he asked himself. Vanessa stood up holding Andrew with concern. Martin's magnified vision crisscrossed the choppy water between the dingy and point.

"Stay calm. Dad will find you," Luke said to himself. He had taken off his heavy tennis shoes and treaded just enough to keep his head above water. Nonetheless, he was beginning to tire. He faced the island and noticed that the current was carrying him away from the point but closer to *Precise Intuition*. Periodically, he raised one arm out of the water and circled with his hand, the sign his dad taught him for a swimmer in distress.

"There he is!" Martin said as he saw Luke's arm flaying intermittingly amongst the swells.

"Good boy, keep that arm up," Martin said.

"Vanessa, I want you to take the binoculars and keep your eyes on Luke at all times. You'll see his arm just above the water. Ill start the engine and raise the anchor." Martin handed the binoculars to Vanessa.

"Do you see him? Do you see him?"

"Yes. Yes, I can see him," Vanessa replied.

"Keep your eyes on him," Martin said as he bent down to turn the key. He pushed the glow plug and studied the second hand on his watch. After twenty-five seconds he pushed the engine start button. The motor did not start. He pushed the throttle to fifty percent, turned the key again, pushed the choke button again, and studied his watch for another agonizing half a minute.

"What's wrong?" Vanessa implored.

"Just keep your eyes on him!" Martin yelled. He reached for the engine start button again and pushed firmly. The motor did not start. Martin tried to remain calm and trouble shoot as another urge started to build in him.

"Vanessa, keep your eyes on Luke. I cannot get the engine started. I'm going to swim for him. Try to start the engine. If not, radio for help. Then pull the anchor and unfurl the jib and set sail for Isaac in the Zodiac. Then come for us," Martin explained as he removed his clothes.

Martin took the binoculars from Vanessa, established Luke's position, considered the direction and power of the waves, chose a line to swim through the chop, and dove over the side of *Precise Intuition*.

Luke could no longer keep his hand twirling as the waves pushed him by *Precise Intuition* 550 meters seaward. He raised one arm and then the other as the chop closed in around him saying,

"Stay calm; dad is coming," over and over again to himself.

Martin swam fast to rescue his son. He arms took long pulls through the rough water and his legs paddled with a strength he had never felt before.

"Keep going. Don't look. Just keep going," he said to himself.

A large swell sideswiped Martin, throwing off his cadence. He stopped, took a few steady breaths, identified his position, made a slight adjustment, and them plunged through the next swell. After a few more strokes his mind went clear and he felt completely at one with his body, an enfleshed spirit reaching for a rescue.

Vanessa held the glow button down with both thumbs. After thirty seconds she pressed the engine start button. The motor did not start. Descending the steps in the companion way, Vanessa stopped at the nav table and turned on the radio. It was set at sixteen, the emergency distress station. Something seemed out of place.

"Stay there," she commanded Andrew, who sat alertly.

She went back up the steps and thought about the directions Martin had left. If she let the anchor go and didn't unfurl the jib sail fast enough the boat would be wrecked near White's Landing. Assuming she did trim the sail correctly, she could reach Andrew in the dingy but then would have grave difficulty getting to Martin and Luke by beating into the wind.

Deciding the engine was vital to their safety, the item that was out of place near the navigation table started to emerge. She went through an "engine starting checklist" in her mind. Turn the battery switch to both, meaning the two batteries, to start the engine. The starter needed to draw from both batteries to have the amps needed for ignition.

"That's it," Vanessa said. She rushed down below. The dial was pointed to the house battery. She turned the knob to "Both". Vanessa climbed the steps rapidly and turned the key. She pushed the glow button and, after a pause, the engine start button. The motor turned over and revved to life.

Running to the bow, Vanessa reached for a fender and tied it to the anchor line quickly. She reached down to remove the rope from the cleat but it wouldn't budge. She ran to the stern, guided by the life line, jumped into the cockpit and throttled down and pushed the gear into forward. The boat slowly started moving toward the anchor line as Vanessa ran back to the bow.

The wind stopped gusting but the swells it had churned out kept pushing the dingy farther and farther away. Isaac could see the island but lost sight of the boat in the distance and approaching darkness. He cupped his hands around his mouth and yelled,

"Mom, Mom!" He thought, "Why didn't I call for mom before? She's always there when I need her.

"Mom, Mom!" Isaac cried.

"Father, Father!" Luke pleaded wearily as his sinking body reached for the sky. He was submerged by another swell and gasped for a new breath after it passed.

"Father, Father," Luke mumbled once more, unable to lift his hand above his head.

Martin swam forward, picked up and dropped by the swells. He stretched out one arm, cupped the ocean in his hands, and pushed through. Then the next arm lifted, dove forward, and fell back. He turned his head and shoulders for a breath every three strokes. His legs began to burn with lactic acid. He knew he was kicking too hard and the muscles demanded more oxygen than could be supplied. He knew he needed to let his arms do the work. He also felt time was running out, so he kicked even harder. Soon after, his legs started to feel heavy and his lungs began to tighten.

Vanessa dropped the anchor line into the water and glided along the edge of the boat. She reached the stern, took the wheel of *Precise Intuition* and pushed the throttle full ahead. The bow cut through the water fast and true. The orange life jacket worn by Isaac appeared off the port side. Soon Vanessa heard his cries. She pulled off on the throttle and went into neutral. The dingy gently bumped into the side of the sailboat.

"Mom, Mom!" Isaac cried.

"Isaac, are you okay?" Vanessa asked.

"Yes, I'm okay, Mom."

"Hand me the rope in the bow." Isaac crawled to the front of the zodiac and grabbed the rope, stood, and handed it to his mother.

"Hold onto the side while I tie this off," Vanessa said.

"Where's dad?" Isaac asked as he climbed onto *Precise Intuition*. Vanessa embraced him saying,

"Sit down. Sit down," as she pushed the throttle forward and turned the wheel. "Go get me the big flashlight."

The light blue sky that had lain over the dark blue sea all day long gradually, imperceptibly dimmed. The height of the wind swell also diminished. Martin stopped, unable to make another stroke. Luke gasped for what he thought would be his last breath. Martin kicked his feet and pushed himself up, looking in one direction. Then Martin thrust himself up again on another bearing.

"Luke, Luke!" Martin yelled, turned, pivoted again and lifted above the chop shouting, "Luke, Luke!"

When the boy heard his father's voice, his sinking heart revived. His limbs strengthened. He took a deep breath and yelled,

"Dad!"

Martin heard his son's voice and swam upwind. The current carried Luke toward his outstretched hands.

"Sorry, Dad," Luke said as he grasped onto his father's shoulders.

"You made it, son. Good boy, good boy," Martin said as twilight turned to night.

The Long Point Light cast its bright beam over the dark water every six seconds.

"Take the wheel and steer for the light," Vanessa said to Isaac as she went below. She switched on the running lights near the navigation table. The port bow light shone red, the starboard side green. Then she took a sweater, went back up the companion way steps with Andrew following behind, and reached the cockpit.

"Here, put this on." Isaac, completely absorbed with the task at hand, didn't respond but kept his eyes on the light.

"Here, put this on," Vanessa said again.

"That's Luke's" Isaac said, fitting the sweater over his head anyway.

"I'll take the wheel. Shine the flashlight over the port side for me," Vanessa ordered.

"Are you warm enough?" Martin asked as Luke held onto his shoulders in the water.

"I'm cold," Luke answered.

"You'll be fine. The water must be seventy degrees. Mom will be coming with the boat," Martin reassured his son as he looked through the swells. The green bow light of *Precise Intuition* glowed over the ocean from a distance.

"There she is!" Martin said. "Why is she so close to the point?" he mumbled to himself.

Vanessa was still looking over the port side as *Precise Intuition* moved precipitously close to the submerged rocks off Long Point. Isaac held the flashlight and aimed it farther out over the water. A sheer cliff reflected back. Vanessa leaned into the steering wheel of the boat as it stopped suddenly, the keel striking a submerged rock.

"No! We've gone aground!" she cried.

Vanessa paused, trying to calm herself and think clearly. Slowly her upset shaking dissipated. Regaining her composure, she reduced power to idle, pulled the transmission lever from forward to reverse and then pushed the power lever back up, this time to full speed. Ten agonizing seconds later, the keel of *Precise Intuition* was free of the underwater bolder. Then, changing direction, Vanessa turned the wheel carefully toward the open sea.

"Thank God!" Vanessa said aloud.

"Let's make another pass. Keep the flashlight over the water on that side," Vanessa said to Isaac. "I'll watch for dad on this side."

"This way, hon," Martin coaxed his wife, who was still far off, as he and Luke were engulfed by another swell. Then the waters parted revealing the red bow light. *Precise Intuition* had completed its turn and was headed straight for them.

Vanessa followed the path of the Long Point Light as it swept over the sea. The white ray hurtled over the chop.

"There they are! Shine the flashlight on this side," she yelled. Vanessa's sighting was confirmed when the beaming faces of her husband and son smiled back. Vanessa turned the stern of *Precise Intuition* into the swells and threw Martin and Luke a yellow life ring.

"Go get some dry towels for your dad and brother," Vanessa said to Isaac and Andrew as she pulled the life ring toward the boat. Martin and Luke were brought alongside as the swim ladder plunged down into the water and shot up with the waves passing under the keel. Timing the swells, Martin guided Luke up the ladder as Vanessa pulled him on board.

"Are you okay?"

"I'm cold," Luke replied as Isaac handed him a towel.

"Why didn't you come back for me?" Luke asked his brother.

"I tried; I tried to row but the waves were too big," Isaac answered.

Martin climbed the swim ladder and stood naked on the deck as Andrew approached sheepishly with a towel. After drying and tying the towel around his waist, Martin embraced his youngest son.

"Get those wet clothes off and get in the shower," Vanessa motioned as she issued the tender directive to Luke.

"I feel like I've been in a washing machine. Mom, after that, I don't think I should have to wash my face again for a month," Luke bargained.

"Let's head for Avalon," Martin suggested to the family as he pushed the transmission forward and throttled *Precise Intuition* toward Moonstone Cove. Then he handed the helm over to Vanessa, descended into the cabin and pressed the hot water shower into service.

After a warm shower the boys, too excited and hungry to sleep, gathered on the deck with their parents under the stars.

"There's the Big Dipper," Andrew said, waving at the sky indiscriminately.

"And you're a little dip," Isaac replied.

"Sounds like things are returning to normal," Vanessa sighed with her arm around Martin's waist.

The three brothers kept talking about all that had happened on the way to Avalon.

"Did you see me? I almost floated to Mexico," Isaac boasted.

"At least you had a boat under you. Try treading water for an hour," Luke responded.

The sea calmed under the clear sky as *Precise Intuition* rounded Casino Point. Jazz music swayed over the bay of Avalon from the terraced balcony of The Casino. Vanessa went below to the navigation table, picked up the radio and set the channel to number twelve.

"This is *Precise Intuition*, a thirty-four foot sailboat, seeking a mooring in Avalon harbor."

"This is the Avalon Harbor Patrol. Proceed to the main harbor entrance and wait," a sober voice replied. Soon a patrol boat rendezvoused with the sailboat near the harbor entrance.

"Look at the phosphorescence," Luke said as he gazed at the prop wash from the harbor patrol boat that led them to their mooring. Vanessa and Luke went to the bow to retrieve the "pick-up" pole, a floating pointed stick to which is attached the bow hawser, as *Precise Intuition* idled to a neutral stillness. Luke fastened the muddy bow line, pulled the spreader to the stern and cleated off the rope with his dad's help.

'Hungry?" Martin asked.

"Yeah, I'm hungry! Food!" the boys replied in chorus.

Martin hailed a water taxi. Soon the family was standing on The Pleasure Pier. Martin and Vanessa walked arm and arm with the boys skipping and circling, darting forward and trailing behind. The family turned on Crescent Avenue, heard the music spilling from The Casino, and flowed into the current of pedestrians.

"Where are we going?" Luke asked.

"The Catalina Country Club," Martin responded. "We just have to find it. Your mom and I went there during our honeymoon. I think it's just up this street, Catalina Avenue."

"It's too far. Dad, can I have a ride on your shoulders," Andrew asked after hiking a few blocks.

"How about a piggy back ride?" Martin asked as he bent his sore legs and offered his stiff neck. Andrew jumped on.

"How much farther?" Isaac asked when the family reached a fork in the road. Just then a golf cart sped to a stop next to them.

"Excuse me. Can you tell us where the Catalina Country Club is?" Vanessa asked.

"Sure," the man said as he turned and pointed over his shoulder with a large hand.

"You're almost there. See the restaurant on top of that hill?"

'Yes," Vanessa replied.

"That's it; you've found it."

"Thank you," Vanessa said as the golf cart took off toward the bay.

The family entered the Catalina Country Club. Even though it was a warm, late summer evening, they were seated next to a crackling log that burned with dancing flames in the dining room fireplace. Feeling underdressed, Martin addressed the boys,

"Take off your hat at the table and put your napkin in your lap. This isn't Raul's Place." Vanessa unfolded her napkin and the boys followed suit. After ordering dinner, the table hushed in a melancholy calm. Underneath Martin's composed exterior, emotions coalesced in a confusing collage.

"Honey, you're quiet tonight." Vanessa commented.

"It's been quite a day," Martin answered with an affirming look at Luke and Isaac. The boys remained subdued not only by hunger but the unspoken standards of conduct imposed on them by their parents in a fancy restaurant. They felt in awe of their dad, who savored the presence of his family in silence.

"Mom handled the boat pretty well today, didn't she?"
The boys nodded.

"Not quite. There may be a few scratches on the keel," Vanessa confessed.

"The most important thing is that we are all safe. We can always repair the keel," Martin replied as dinner was served.

"Let's pray," Vanessa said. Martin spoke the usual blessing but it seemed, to him, to be a superficial request, an inadequate utterance. A pause ensued, the family waiting to hear more.

"Amen," Martin said.

When the rich meal had completed its course, crowned by a sweet dessert, the family left the table and walked back down the hill near the golf course.

"Listen to the frogs; there must be a million of them," Luke said as the long high ribetts and short base croaks rumbled through the canyon. Vanessa drew closer to Martin, who was still more silent than usual as he glanced up at the street signs.

"Looking for something?" Vanessa asked as she reached for her husband's hand.

"Do you remember the church we visited during our honeymoon? I think it is near here."

"Can we go this way?" Luke asked as he reached a fork in the road. The family followed Luke to Beacon Street and saw the bell tower of Saint Catherine's Catholic Church. Martin stopped in his tracks. Studying her husband's face, Vanessa said,

"Let's go to the church; it will only be for a few minutes. Then we'll get back on the boat and go to bed." The tired boys groaned.

"If you want to, why not?" Martin replied.

"This way, boys," Vanessa said, calling her sons back.

When the family reached the church, Martin gazed upon a statue of the Blessed Virgin Mary. Behind the image were yellow Catalina tiles, the same shade as the cupola of The Cathedral of the Immaculate Conception in Mazatlán. The moments passed in silence as Martin remembered.

"I hear the water but where is the fountain?" Isaac asked. Andrew pulled at his dad's side. The family walked into the bougainvillea courtyard and smelled the evening scent of the Hesperia and the heavenly aroma of roses. The boys circled the fountain and peered in at a few coins. They laughed as they reached for the flowing water and deflected the spray toward each other. Vanessa put her finger over her mouth,

"Shh!"

Martin walked to a door in the church and reached for the handle, wondering if it would be open. As Martin crossed the threshold, he felt a sense of welcome like that of greeting an old friend. He genuflected to the tabernacle that resembled The Ark of the Covenant and knelt before the Blessed Sacrament. Luke and Isaac entered through the same portal and knelt on each side of their dad, followed by Andrew.

Joy and sorrow tore Martin's heart from top to bottom as relief gushed forth in tears. Vanessa approached and touched one of Martin's sobbing shoulders. Martin wiped his face and took a deep breath. The boys started to cry as they looked up to their father, who spread his arms over them. Looking at Luke and smiling through the tears, Martin bowed his head saying,

"I could not save my dad, but I rescued my son."

Chapter Twenty-Two
Homecoming in Jalisco

Israel returned to his home in *Los Altos de Jalisco* behind the wheel of a car that he rented in Guadalajara. He drove by the town's plaza, only to find it quiet, still in observance of the afternoon *siesta*. Then he turned on the street leading out to his father's dairy farm. Soon the road bumped before him, sending a plume of dust behind. Gradually, he reached the fence post marking the driveway. In a slow, drawn out flashback, he heard the fatal blast that brought his brother Joaquin, face first, into the ground.

In the tentative seconds before Israel stepped out from the car, his dad, Rodolfo, and his younger brother Abel with his wife, approached. A niece and nephew who had been playing by the pond also drew near and clamored for a ride.

"Welcome home, son," Rodolfo said, greeting Israel with a hand-shake and firm embrace. "Your mother can't wait to see you."

Glancing at the wooden barn, Israel followed his father into the kitchen of the stone house. There he watched his grey-haired mother stir a pot of *pasole* on the stove. Magdalena was now in her late-fifties and her diminishing hearing allowed Israel to walk up beside her.

"Can I stir that for you?"

Magdalena gasped, slapped his arm, and looked at her oldest son for only the second time in nearly twenty years. Then she cried joyfully as Rodolfo held them both with tears in his eyes.

"You must be hungry," she said, wiping her eyes. "Go sit down and I'll bring you some *pasole*."

The cold beer and hot red soup with giant corn kernels and pieces of beef were set before Israel and his father moments after sitting down. Magdalena took a seat to watch her son eat. Israel reached for a handful of cabbage that he placed on top of the soup. Then he heaped on spoons full of onions and radishes, squeezed the juice of two limes, and rubbed fresh Mexican oregano over the *pasole*.

"Where is Socorro?" Israel inquired about his oldest sister, a woman who took care of everyone but neglected herself.

"She has gone to town for a few things."

Magdalena began speaking about the homecoming banquet being held for him the next day: who was coming and from where. To help his memory, she brought pictures, one by one, from the living room. By the time Israel finished his meal, the table was covered with photographs of the family.

Abel excused himself from the table and Israel and Rodolfo followed him out to the barn shortly thereafter. Abel, his wife and children milked the cows as Rodolfo and Israel looked on.

"I'd like to climb the mountain tomorrow," Israel said.

"I'll go with you, son."

After sunset Magdalena showed Israel to his old room- the one he had shared with Joaquin - and which Abel and his wife graciously relinquished for the duration of his visit.

Israel passed a restless night in fitful sleep, punctuated by the howl of coyotes.

With the crow of the rooster Israel awoke to questions, scarcely formulated, that conspired to drive him from bed. Did his tendency to scrutinize his life accompany the approach of his fortieth birthday or was it seeing the man who murdered his brother again? Israel had anticipated his homecoming and now felt the day of reckoning was at hand. Today the rationale for his work would meet reality in the vast space of the hard land and the intimacy of his close knit family. Were the prosperity of the family and his sense of justice worth the toil exacted by a shameful business? Was he really sacrifing himself for the family or had he always used the ideal of the family for himself? And what about Claudia? Where did she fit in? When did he begin to love the woman he began by using?

Unable to remain under the cover of thought or illusion any longer, Israel got up to meet the destined day that only the land might unlock and the family unfold. Israel pulled on his boots thinking about the biblical stories of judgment and looked out the window, his heart beating to the parables of mercy. The light from the rising sun burned his eyes so he looked away. Then the cheerful voice of his father beckoned him. Soon, he was with his dad laboring at the chores on the farm as he did when he was a boy.

Late in the morning, after breakfast, Israel and his dad started their climb up the sacred mountain. Israel followed his dad across a patchy green-gold pasture with cow paddies, through a barbed wire fence and over a muddy creek. Dragonflies flitted before them as Israel thought about how nothing had changed until they came upon some shallow pits with chilies drying in the sun.

"This is new."

"The boys farm them and take them to market in town."

Israel and his dad continued to weave their way along the fields and then began traversing the base of the mountain. Aging father would lead for one stretch before his full-grown son eagerly took over the march at front. Rodolfo stopped occasionally to rest and catch his breath but disguised the behavior by pointing out a novelty along the trail. Israel stole glimpses of his dad's stooping posture.

After climbing for almost two hours, they reached the top of the sacred mountain of their ancestors. The green valley stretched before then with majestic serenity.

"It's still worth the climb," Israel said.

"Yes," his dad responded with a smile, shaking a little from the exertion.

"Dad, do you ever follow the trail around to the other side of the mountain?"

"The trail ends a few yards ahead."

Israel picked his way through the narrowing trail and thorny brush. Then he cut a path away from the side of the steep mountain top's ridge. His dad followed.

"Why do you want to go back here?"

"I have something to show you."

After another quarter hour of struggle that left both men scratched, they reached the other side of the mountain. The plateau beneath them was arid.

"We'll have to improve that trail if you're going to keep an eye on all your land," Israel suggested.

"What?" his dad asked.

"The land on this side of the mountain now belongs to us."

"What do you mean? What are you saying?"

"The import-export business has been profitable."

"What will we do with so much land?"

"Three hundred head of cattle to start. You think you can teach Abel and the rest what they need to know?"

His dad took off his cowboy hat, scratched his head, and said,

"I'll teach them."

"Dad, I want you to tell Abel about it before the fiesta today."

"I will. I will."

"We'd better turn back now or we'll be late," Israel said as he began to lead the way down the sacred mountain as far as the last creek. Then he followed his dad the rest of the way home.

Later, after a shower and shave, and after welcoming his extended family, Israel sat down for the banquet at one end of a long table facing his father. Outside the dining room, but still visible to their parents, portable chairs began to fill with Rodolfo and Magdalena's twenty-eight grandchildren. Israel's only older sibling, Socorro, with the help of his nieces, brought the food to the tables in both rooms. Then she made the first call for everyone to be seated and the prayer to begin. During the meal, Socorro did not sit for long. When she was not getting up to check on the children, she brought more steak and chilies, beans and rice, tamales and tacos to the table.

"Pass the salsa," one of Israel's brothers, an auto mechanic in town, requested. Israel passed the spicy sauce to Abel and followed its progress down the table as his brother received it with finely crevassed, oil-stained hands. Israel listened as his brother, dressing a taco with the salsa, spoke across the table about his children's education to another brother with spectacles who taught Spanish-American Literature and History at the University of Guadalajara.

Israel smiled as he turned his gaze on the profiles of his three beautiful youngest sisters, now married with children of their own. Sitting next to Israel, and wanting desperately to speak to him, were Abel and another brother, Efrain, who lived on a corner of his father's land. They discreetly inquired about the land on the other side of the mountain. Israel remained purposefully vague, much to their annoyance.

After the meal, Socorro poured coffee as the plates were removed from the table. Then Israel, tapping the side of his cup with a spoon, called for everyone's attention. One of his nephews brought a bag filled with identical gift-wrapped boxes. The eleven boxes were passed to each brother and brother-in-law. Israel nodded to his father.

"Go ahead and open them," Rodolfo said.

Ripping the paper and pulling at the boxes, each man sorted through tissue paper to find a pair of silver spurs. A few of the men studied the gift quizzically. The rest spun the silver stars and tested the metal and sharpness. Each man, with the exception of Rodolfo, searched for the meaning of such a gift. Finally, Israel stood up and said,

"We have acquired the flat land on the other side of the mountain. It is my hope, that with your hard work, the family will return to ranching. We'll buy cattle and horses in the fall. But before that, there are irrigation ditches to dig, alfalfa seeds to sow and stalls to build. The family will prosper and the land will provide opportunity for you and your children."

"You mean no more milking cows?" Efrain interrupted.

"You can if you want," Israel retorted.

"Yah,Yah! Ride'em cowboy! Yah!" his dad hollered as he slapped his hands on the top of his legs. The rest of the family laughed with merriment at the patriarch's outburst.

Finishing their coffee, the guests took leave to return to their own homes. Israel, together with his dad, Abel and Efrain moved to the living room and began drinking the brandy and smoking the cigars that he had brought for the occasion.

As the moon shed its silver glow, Israel presented his father with another gift. This time Rodolfo carefully removed the paper from the gift, a book. As he turned it over in his calloused palms, he identified the volume as the biography of Hernan Cortés, the very book he himself had given his son when he left home so many years ago.

"A friend once told me that I am no Cortés," Israel said as he looked around the old familiar room, "but it is good to return to Mexico triumphant after my exile." Then he gazed into the distance. With the chime of the grandfather clock, Israel honed his hazel eyes on his dad and brothers, set down his drink and extinguished his cigar. Gazing into the distance again, Israel said quietly,

"I want goats and sheep to graze together in the highlands. And, let the weeds grow with the wheat and corn."

Chapter Twenty-Three
Together in Avalon

Robins beat the dew-covered ground as skylarks sang to greet the dawn. The sun was still behind the ribbed mountains of Catalina Island when Father John stepped sprightly from the rectory. He passed the fountain as he crossed the courtyard, anticipating the Sunday gathering of the faithful in the silent morning air. The padre took out a key to unlock the church but, when he pulled on the handle, discovered that the door to the house of prayer was already open.

"I must have forgotten last night," Father John gently berated himself. "I guess I still haven't gotten used to locking the church. Pity that a few people spoil it for everyone else. Let it go." Then he willed the easy remembrance of last night's jazz festival.

"That was good fun," the padre said to himself as he thought of his dear friends, the Harmonds. He called to mind their seats in the *high topper* section of the Grand Ballroom at The Casino as the brass bands turned out jazz tunes for all of Avalon to hear.

"What a night," the padre said with a smile. Then the expression of happiness receded as another emotion stirred his heart. He remembered praying for the young woman coming down off of speed.

"What was her name?" he asked himself. "Judy, yes, Judy, that's it."

The Catalina hospital had been open all night. Connie, the nurse who cared for Judy, checked on her patient as she finished her twelve-hour shift. Judy sat with slumped shoulders on the edge of the bed with her backpack and the pink blanket Fr. John had placed on her shoulders.

"Do you want to keep it?" Connie asked.

"Yes. Can I?" Judy said with unsure optimism.

"Of Course. Are you returning home today?"

"Yes. I miss my girls. I pick them up at my mom's tonight," Judy responded as she shuffled and fussed over the straps of her backpack.

"I need you to stay still for a moment while I take your blood pressure." Judy felt the cuff expand and tighten around her slender arm as Connie listened to her pulse with a stethoscope and monitored the pressure with a gauge.

"148 over 86."

"How am I?"

"Your blood pressure is still high but lower than yesterday," Connie replied, drawing out the last word.

"But?" Judy asked as she squirmed on the end of the bed.

"Using drugs does not help you or your family."

"I'm trying to stop," Judy said as she pulled the pink blanket to her chest.

"You need to go to a Narcotics Anonymous group or Crystal Meth Anonymous and meet people who have been through what you are going through. You are not alone. There is hope. I know you can do it."

"What is hope?" Judy asked with a discouraged sigh.

Connie thought about the question as she sat on the edge of the bed next to Judy.

"Hope is like the view we have when we look at the horizon, the future, with faith, with trust in God and with trust in ourselves."

"I would like to trust again."

"You can. Listen. Let's check you out from here and I'll give you the names and phone numbers of a few N.A. groups near you if you promise to use them," Connie offered.

Judy nodded, the color starting to return to her pale face.

"Good," Connie affirmed. "I'll walk you back toward town at least as far as the church."

"Father John's church?" Judy asked.

"Saint Catherine's. Would you like to join me?" Connie invited. "You know, something I always experience, is that after prayer I feel more hopeful. I can't explain it. Maybe we'll ask Father John why."

"Yes, ahh, yes, I would like that," Judy responded.

When Father John walked into the church, he saw Martin and Vanessa sitting with the boys in the first pew.

"Good morning," Father John said. Martin approached the priest and asked,

"Ahh, Father, do you have a minute?"

"Is this for confession?"

"Yes," Martin replied.

"I usually do not hear confessions on Sunday but," the padre said, looking at his watch, "we still have time. Follow me." Father John led Martin into the sanctuary and set two seats across from each other in a corner.

"Sit here for a minute. I'll be right back," Father John said as he withdrew into the sacristy. A few moments later he returned wearing a long white alb with a purple stole over his shoulders. He sat down in the chair facing Martin and traced the image of the cross on his forehead, chest and shoulders saying,

"In the name of the Father, and of the Son, and of the Holy Spirit. How long has it been since your last confession?"

"A long time," Martin replied.

"Has it been more than five years?"

Martin nodded affirmatively.

"More that ten years?"

"Yes. I don't know where to begin," Martin said.

"Welcome back. This is a celebration of God's mercy. What brings you here after so many years?" the priest asked with a tender smile. The tears welled up in Martin's eyes.

"Yesterday I almost lost my son. He almost drowned. I have been angry with God for so long for taking my dad away from me. Now I am grateful my sons are alive." The tears flowed as he sat quietly. After a moment, Martin brushed the tears away and said,

"It's been so long. I don't know where to start."

"You have made a fine beginning. We usually examine our conscience and name each sin and how many times it has occurred."

"Okay," Martin said as he looked down, searching his memory like someone going through an old chest of drawers.

"I haven't been going to church with my family as much as I should. I haven't visited my mom or talked to her for a while. I get consumed by work and forget everyone else." Then Martin glanced up only to look down more firmly. He took a deep breath and confessed,

"I once transported drugs across the border. It was a long time ago."

Then Father John, wishing he could say more but refraining due to the time said,

"For your penance, either visit your mother or go to a drug rehabilitation center and make a donation. Do you understand your penance?"

"Yes," Martin said with a sigh of relief.

"Do you remember your Act of Contrition?"

"I think so, in Spanish." Martin renewed his sorrow for his sins. Then the padre extended his hand over Martin's head and said,

"God, the Father of Mercies, through the death and resurrection of his Son, has reconciled the world to himself and sent the Holy Spirit among us for the forgiveness of sins. Through the ministry of the Church, may God grant you pardon and peace." Then Martin was absolved of his sins in the name of the Trinity.

"Thank you," Martin said. "Sometimes it is difficult for me to be a good father to my sons. My dad died when I was young and sometimes I don't know how. This is such a relief for me. I feel you have helped me to be a better father. Thank you," Martin said as he rose up to go.

"Give thanks to the Lord, for he is good," the priest said as he looked up, "The reply is 'his mercy endures forever.'"

"His mercy endures forever," Martin said with a smile as he returned to his family.

Before the padre could stand up, Judy was sitting down across from him. Judy made the sign of the cross and confessed,

"I have used drugs."

"Is it your intention not to use drugs again?" Father John asked.

"Yes, but it's so hard. I've also doubted my faith and lost hope. I'm going to try to go to church. If God would only help me, I could stop," Judy said as her voice trailed off into a whisper.

"The first step toward liberation is the conviction that with God's help it is possible. God will help you but you must choose to help yourself by not using drugs. For your penance, pray about joining a narcotics anonymous group," the priest directed. Judy peeked up again before putting her head back down.

"And now your Act of Contrition."

"I don't know it, Father," Judy said.

"Please try to learn it. Repeat after me. Lord Jesus, you restored sight to the blind."

"Lord Jesus, you restored sight to the blind."

"You healed the sick," the padre said with a smile.

"You healed the sick," Judy repeated.

"You forgave the sinful women," Father John said more slowly.

"You forgave the sinful women," Judy said with more confidence.

"And after Peter's denial, confirmed him in the faith."

"And after Peter's denial, confirmed him in the faith."

"I am sorry for my sins," the priest said.

"I am sorry for my sins," the penitent replied.

Father John extended his hand over Judy and spoke the words of absolution. Judy rose and walked to the second pew, taking a seat with Connie behind Martin and his family. Father John disappeared through a door in the sanctuary.

People started to arrive and, by nine o'clock, the church was almost full. The bells rang warmly as the cantor stood near the organist. The large doors of the church opened as sunshine poured through. The padre processed down the center isle toward the altar like Jesus' triumphal entry into Jerusalem.

Luke, Isaac and Andrew had been talking under the volume of the opening hymn. When the music stopped, their voices continued. Vanessa's face flushed as she told the boys to be quiet. She looked apologetically at the priest and asked herself why they had sat in the front row. The boys made the sign of the cross and Father John greeted the people, many of whom were still coming into the church.

During the opening rites, Martin marveled at God's ways, how indeed He writes straight with crooked lines. The proclamation of the gospel from Mathew 5:34-48 brought Martin to his feet with the rest of the community.

Father John started expounding on the gospel passage just proclaimed where Jesus commands his followers to love their enemies and pray for those who persecute them. Expanding on the message, he read the following quote from St. Thomas More, the patron of lawyers, statesmen and politicians, who was beheaded on London Bridge in 1535:

> Bear no malice or evil will toward any living person. For either the person is good or wicked. If the person is good and I hate him, then I am wicked.
>
> If he is wicked, either he will amend and die good and go to God, or live wickedly and die wickedly and go to the devil. And then let me remember that if this person be saved, he will not fail (if I am saved too, as I trust to be) to love me very heartily, and I shall then, in like manner love him.
>
> And why should I now, then, hate one for this while who shall hereafter love me forever, and why should I be now, then, an enemy to one with whom I shall in time be coupled in eternal friendship? And on the other side, if this person will continue to be wicked and be damned, then is there such outrageous eternal sorrow before him that I may well think myself a deadly cruel wretch if I would not now rather pity their pain than malign their person.

After the homily, everyone professed their faith and interceded with God for the needs of the Church and the world. The people knelt as the Roman Catholic ritual continued toward its climactic moments. The priest held his hands over the bread and wine and invoked the Holy Spirit at the consecration. Then the priest spoke the words Jesus spoke at the Last Supper,

"Take this, all of you, and eat it: this is my body which will be given up for you." Father John genuflected. Then he said,

"At the end of the meal, knowing that he was to reconcile all things in himself by the blood of his cross...." The priest raised the chalice above the altar and continued,

"Take this, all of you, and drink from it: this is the cup of my blood, the blood of the new and everlasting covenant. It will be shed for you and for all so that sins may be forgiven. Do this in memory of me."

Praying on behalf of the people, the priest arrived at the final doxology expressing praise to God. The people stood and responded in a song-filled acclamation and the Lord's Prayer.

"Let us offer each other the sign of peace," Fr. John said. Martin kissed Vanessa on the cheek modestly and embraced his sons firmly. Then he turned around. Judy stood timidly looking at Martin. Their eyes met and their outstretched hands clasped each other.

"Peace be with you," said Martin. To which Judy responded,

"Peace be with you."

Then Judy, Martin's family, and the rest of the community filed out of the pews in procession to the altar. They each received the one real, true and sacramental body and blood of Christ and returned to their seats and knelt. Song gave way to silence.

During Holy Communion Martin experienced a deep sense of healing and gratitude that permeated his whole being. Judy felt a new sense of belonging that filled her with hope. But even with such consolation, she still yearned for more. For as yet, she did not know how to wait humbly in faith for the Lord to lead her along the thread of peace into the tapestry of glory. Luke, with all the innocence and trust of childhood, detected the almost imperceptible whisper of contemplation and became conscious of his connection to the mystery of life like a syllable of The Word.

Isaac and Andrew beamed, not knowing why, the filament of their souls burning with joy in the firmament of heaven. The Spirit led Father John to have only one desire, that of offering himself with Jesus. In the same instant, he was conformed to the suffering and glorified Christ. Vanessa's spiritual hunger for the strength needed to meet the future adventures of her family was satisfied like that of a wayfarer receiving food for the journey. Connie, secure in the faith and knowledge of God's love for her, rejoiced in gratitude for all God's gifts.

After the final blessing the priest said,

"Go in peace to love and serve the Lord."

Joyful chatter and glorious music overflowed from the church into the courtyard where the people visited after the liturgy.

Judy hugged Father John, had breakfast with Connie and departed on the *Sea Horse Express* for San Pedro. Martin and Vanessa's family had brunch, picked up their anchor, and set sail on *Precise Intuition* for the mainland.

Three weeks later, Father John received a postcard with an image of The Cathedral of The Immaculate Conception in Mazatlán. The words, *free from original sin*, though printed small near the yellow domes of the Cathedral, caught his eye.

"Original sin," the priest paused with a sigh, "that explains a lot." He turned the card over and was delighted to read,

"Dear Fr. John, we celebrated Mass with Grandma. Thank you." Scribbled under the farewell, in each of their own hands, were the names Martin, Vanessa, Luke, Isaac and Andrew. The padre was moved to the point of prayer for the family, a community of life and a school of love.

Fr. John carried the post card into the living room and placed it on top of what he called his *beautiful mess* of pictures: hundreds of photographs sent by individuals the priest shared life with - people trying to keep in touch, asking for prayer, and expressing gratitude - all set before a small and graceful statue of Mary, the Mother of God.

About the Author

Robert Capone is a fourth generation Californian who has made his home on the state's Pacific shore. As a waterman with numerous adventures along the Baja California coast and as a student of Latino culture with many trips to mainland Mexico, he is uniquely qualified to bring the currents of this vibrant and emerging region to the recreational reader.

Robert has a master's degree in religion from St. John's Seminary in Camarillo and a bachelor of arts in business economics from The University of San Diego. Robert was ordained a priest in the Roman Catholic Church in the Jubilee Year 2000. The triumphs and tragedies of the families to whom he ministers find expression in his writing. The interplay between a contemplative and active life gracefully permeate the dramatic pages of this, his first novel, *A Remote but Frequented Shore*.

Author Photograph on back cover by H.M. DeCruyenaere

Printed in the United States
73926LV00003B/292-303